....A perfect murder mystery....

~Dana Point Times

In a "suspenseful... smooth, compulsive" read, national bestselling and award winning author Maria Grazia Swan, delivers a "can't-put-it-down kind of read, almost like a dream/nightmare that won't stop"

~Italophile Book Reviews

GEMINI MOON

Cover design by Debbie Coleman
www.ImagineThat-Design.biz

Formatting by Debora Lewis
arenapublishing.org

ISBN-13: 978-1535548700
ISBN-10: 1535548703

GEMINI MOON

Maria Grazia Swan

To Mary Ann Dennison–
True Friend and Astrologer Extraordinaire

October 1933 - April 2014

R.I.P.

ONE

I tend to do my crying in the car.

On this starless, moonless night, without a car or a Beatles song to cry to, I spent my last night in Florence, Italy, as anonymous as any other tourist.

An outsider in my motherland.

I stamped my feet on the old bridge, trying to keep warm. Memories of Nick and our last time in Italy filled my head and pained my heart.

The glow of a candle caught my attention. On impulse, I crossed Ponte Vecchio and walked toward the man sitting by the candle, the heels of my boots clicking against the quarry slabs. The stranger didn't move. He stared at the worn book that lay in front of him on a table covered in red velvet.

Around us, Florence's underground nighttime economy thrived. Peddlers displayed their wares and called out to the tourists on the walkway. Most of the sellers were African and donned colorful native cottons. The smart ones wore overcoats.

The candle flickered in the wind and cast leaping shadows on the man's bony face. Thick lashes framed his eyes and a deep furrow crossed his forehead. I stood, intrigued yet hesitant. Cold sneaked down the back of my neck and spine. I pulled the collar of my mohair coat up to my chin. The fuzzy wool chafed my skin.

"What are you selling?" I asked in Italian.

He focused his dark eyes on me. Their intensity reminded me of my friend Ruby's.

"I am an astrologer." He returned his attention to his book.

"You are?" I felt silly, not sure why. "Quanto costa?"

"Ten euros." About $15. A pittance.

"Va bene."

He pointed to a stool. I sat, then rested the plastic bag that contained a gift for Ruby against the leg of the table. I pressed down two bills beside his candle.

The astrologer held a pencil over a square sheet of white paper.

"When were you born and where?" He spoke Italian with an unusual accent.

"Where are you from?"

He frowned at my question.

I squirmed on the edge of the stool so much my foot kicked the bag. It fell over, and a corner of the turquoise silk shirt peeked out.

"Madrid." He doodled, waiting for my information.

Something didn't feel right. I fought the urge to get up and leave. "December twenty-ninth, 1952," I said.

"Where?"

"L.A. I mean, Los Angeles, California."

"Los Ángeles." He repeated the name as if it were a prayer.

The paper showed a circle divided into segments, like a wagon wheel. He scribbled in one of the sections. My previous charts had been done by computers. I almost wished he had my birthdate. The one I'd given him was Ruby's.

Tanned fingers held the pencil the way an artist held a brush. He scrawled numbers, consulted his book and transcribed his findings on the wagon wheel.

He sat back, his thin lips stretched in a smile. "You are a Capricorn with Gemini moon, Mercury in Sagittarius. Fascinating."

That smile. I shivered.

"Happy childhood." His eyes searched my face. "I see...a sibling. A sister, perhaps?"

Ruby was an only child. "No, I'm afraid not, no sister or brother."

Did he sense the triumph in my voice, my wanting to prove him wrong? With his fingertips on the table, he leaned back so his face was outside the circle of light. Then he leaned forward again to study the paper.

The gold stud in his right earlobe reflected the gleam of the candle.

How old was he? I couldn't tell.

"Close bond with your mother. Only child, you say. Still...she could have lost a child..."

"You mean a miscarriage?"

"More like a stillbirth, an abortion, lots of anger, pain..."

By now I regretted my lie. I was tempted to tell him to keep the money and forget the whole thing, but my lips refused to form the words. His voice seemed muffled. I felt disoriented, the way I would after an unexpected kiss.

"Twenty-two degrees Venus conjunct Mars. Very active love life." He sounded amused.

Was he reading my mind?

"At a young age, fifteen, maybe sixteen...am I correct?"

I remembered Ruby's smoky voice: "Hell, I gave it away before my sophomore year."

And my reply: "Ruby, at that age I hadn't even been kissed."

"I would say that's your problem," she'd said.

I agreed. We laughed and toasted good sex and bad men.

"Correct?" The astrologer urged me on.

"Yes, you're right." I pulled my collar a little higher. I felt more bewildered than cold, but didn't want him to know. "Can you tell all that from a birthdate?"

In the background, someone played a guitar. A violin joined in.

"You are a very creative individual. You could be an artist, an architect?" He paused. "A dress designer?"

Ruby had been a fashion editor before her accident.

"You're good."

He didn't seem to be listening. He grasped the edge of the table with such force the velvet cover slid toward him. The candle tilted. Strands of gray hair peeked out amid the black at his temples.

"Pluto opposing Mars. Venus conjunction." He shoved his chair back. His hand hit the chart. The paper became airborne then landed in front of me. Craning his neck, he stood, almost hovering over me, anger distorting his features.

"Vattene. Go away."

"What?"

He pointed to the bills on the table. "Take your money and go. Now."

I jumped to my feet, knocking over the stool. I turned to walk away. His hand grabbed my shoulder.

"Take your money. Take this chart. The chart of a dead woman." He let go of me as if the touch had scorched his fingers.

Angry tears threatened my eyes. I clutched the paper and money against my chest and ran. I ran to the end of the bridge, ignoring the vendors and bystanders. I ran until Ponte Vecchio became a series of blurry lights and dark store windows. A bicycle grazed me; the rider swore.

I leaned against the cold stones of an ancient palace and caught my breath. Unbelievable. I looked at the crumpled paper and the ten euros. Well, Ruby Russell, you got yourself a free chart.

The chart of a dead woman.

I put the money in the inside pocket of my coat. I'd left Ruby's gift under the astrologer's table. Too bad. Nothing could make me go back there. I'd get her something else tomorrow, but it was my last night here. My last night in Italy. I quivered from the inside out. I wouldn't let a lunatic intimidate me.

I marched back to the bridge.

Ponte Vecchio now looked deserted. The few remaining vendors were packing their merchandise. Where was that man?

I reached the center of the bridge. No table, no candle and no astrologer. I looked in all directions, searching for the stranger with Ruby's eyes.

Nothing.

When I asked one of the peddlers, he shook his head and offered me some knock-off designer sunglasses at a bargain price. Next to him a tall, thin man proudly showed off row after row of Rolexes.

"L'astrologo, era li." Even after over twenty-five years in the States, my Italian was still good. Plus, I underscored my words with my hands, local style, something that always made Nick smile. "You must have noticed him. He had a candle on the table..."

I didn't like the way they stared at me. "No," one after another they told me. They had been selling on the bridge for years, and none knew of any astrologer. Ever.

I touched the crisp paper in my coat pocket. Okay, that was real. I hadn't imagined the strange astrologer.

I headed back to the hotel with Ruby's chart.

Exclusive boutiques lined Borgo San Jacobo. The street, with its row of brightly lit windows, gave me comfort, and I welcomed the sight of Hotel Lungarno's marquee. All I wanted now was to get out of my clothes, take a long, hot shower and forget the disturbing confrontation.

The crystalline sound of the bell brought Primo, the bellman, to the front desk before the door swished closed behind me.

"Signora York. I had hoped to be able to say goodbye."

More likely he hoped to make sure he collected his tip. No, that wasn't it. Primo was a dear man, not very smart, but nice. The management kept the bright ones for the day shift. Primo was always willing to help, even when no help was needed. He gave me a big smile, showing his chipped front tooth. A souvenir, he'd told me, from his brief, but glorious boxing career—at least according to him. I had my doubts. Short and skinny, he wasn't built like a boxer.

"There was a telephone call for you."

"A phone call?" Oh, no. I wasn't expecting a phone call. The announcement set my paranoia in motion, and with good reason. The last time I received an unexpected call while out of the States, my life as I knew it ended. Who would call me on my last night away? It had to be an emergency. What else? My American cell phone didn't work in Europe, so I always gave out the hotel front-desk line for emergencies.

Primo may have sensed my concern, because he attempted to give me his translation of the caller's conversation. It seemed to involve chocolate? Surely not.

"The name, what was the name of the caller?" I pressed.

"Well..." He scratched his nose. I could see he was trying hard to remember. "Well, it was a signora."

"Thank you, Primo. Good night." Wonderful. Just wonderful. I'd have been a thousand times better off not learning anyone called. Might as well go up to my room and phone everyone I knew. I wouldn't get any sleep. Not until I found out who called and why.

I walked from to the elevator and pushed the button. Voices and the clinking of glasses came from the downstairs bar. For a minute, I was tempted to take the lift down and try to forget about the phone call. No. Better go to my room. I'd had enough thrills for one night.

I stepped into the elevator.

Primo came toward me. "Signora, signora, mi ricordo. I remember. Rubee. Rubee was the name."

I felt for the astrologer's euros in my pocket, pulled out the crinkled bills and handed them to Primo. He bowed to me for the third time. I was grateful when the door slid shut.

Ruby had called again. We'd spoken only a few days ago. I smiled. A phone call from the dead woman. Oh, Ruby, great timing. Then again, I wasn't surprised. She was the only person I knew who would call me halfway around the world just to chat. I kept telling her she needed to find a job or a cause.

I tried phoning her back using the room phone. All international circuits were busy, and I was oh so tired. Maybe she wanted me to bring back some Swiss chocolate? That I could do, since I was flying home tomorrow. Whatever else she wanted to tell me would have to wait.

The shower felt so wonderful. I lingered under the hot water. Afterward I felt much better. I turned on the television to CNN. Results from the 2006 Torino Winter Olympics, another car bombing in Baghdad...I clicked it off. My coat lay where I'd thrown it on the bed. I didn't want to carry it on the plane. I would pack it and wear a suit instead. Nick had always done the packing for us. I always unpacked. This was my second visit to Florence since his death four years ago.

Time healed? I missed him more every day.

I fell asleep thinking about my son. Kyle promised to pick me up at LAX.

A knock on the bedroom door woke me.

"Un momento. I'm coming." I threw the robe over my shoulders and flung the door open.

The young man smiled. "Good morning, Mrs. York. Your breakfast."

He placed the tray on the table by the window, removed the white linen covering the plate and opened the roll-up shutters to let the daylight in. "I hope you've enjoyed your stay."

I tipped him. "Can you send for my luggage in about forty-five minutes?"

"Of course. I will also arrange for your transport to the train station."

As usual, the simple breakfast was just what I wanted.

Hot coffee with those baseball-sized rolls so common in Italy. I couldn't wait to bite into their golden crust. I wouldn't have time to look at the newspaper, but I could take it with me to read on the train to Milan.

Steam rose from the delicate porcelain cup. I tore a roll in half, munched on it and went to the window to look at the Arno, one of the many charms that kept me coming back to Hotel Lungarno. The views pleased me, as did, of course, the endearing memories that embraced my heart every moment I spent here. Nick and I always requested this room when we visited Florence. It had become a tradition. Cuddling in the old-fashioned high bed. Waking to the voice of coaches calling the strokes to the rowers practicing on the water. All the windows faced the river, and by stretching my neck I could see Ponte Vecchio. That was one sight I wasn't anxious to see today, although I would feed the fish.

Every morning I opened the window and dropped crumbled bread into the water. Soon, hundreds of fish of all shapes and sizes jumped and fought for the morsels. Other guests did it too. No doubt the reason for the extra rolls. One morning, when Nick was still with me, I leaned out to take a picture of the fish feeding and noticed one of the kitchen staff sitting on the ledge of a lower window—fishing. I was so angry I threatened to throw the camera at him. He disappeared inside. I didn't catch him doing it again. Nick laughed so hard he had tears in his eyes. He took my picture by the window. This window.

I opened the single pane of glass. A smoky smell lingered in the freezing air and drifted into the room. Dozens of chimneys dotted the red-tiled roofs. Even the clouds had the tinge of sooted snow. Winter in Florence. I pulled my robe tight against the chilled air and dispensed the small pieces of bread to the hungry mouths below. The last breakfast I would serve them until next year. I leaned out to see if they were nibbling.

Beneath my window, a billowing piece of turquoise

fabric floated atop the gray waters. I leaned even further out to catch a better look.

It couldn't be. My heart raced. Ruby's shirt? I closed the window without looking back.

TWO

In the cramped lavatory of the airplane, I said, "It's back to hell" to the foggy mirror. An expression I'd picked up from Ruby. It didn't matter where she came from or what awaited her, her mantra for every homecoming was always "back to hell."

Kyle looked so handsome and sophisticated in a dark suit I'd never seen before. What appeared so different about him? He seemed thinner, more mature, although I'd been gone just three weeks. Dio mio, his resemblance to Nick was uncanny. "Always something there to remind me," as the song went. Would I ever get used to it?

"Mom, you made it. Welcome back." He hugged me.

I lingered in the embrace, taking in the familiar scent of his aftershave.

Kyle grabbed my bag. "What did you put in here, lead?"

One of our old jokes.

"Did you do something? You look..."

"My hair, Mom. I had to lighten it. The part called for a blonde."

"Oh!" My son the actor. I had to smile.

Passengers crowded around the luggage carousel. Lots of tired eyes and sleepy faces. "Did you stop by the house while I was away? I know it's silly, but I worry about Flash. Then I see her and all is well and promise myself I won't do that again."

"No. Sorry. We've been shooting in Palm Springs. We're behind schedule." He ran his fingers through his straight hair, now cut short. He seemed tired.

"I'm sure Mrs. Russell has everything under control."

He patted my arm, his eyes alight with mischief.

I always suspected him of having a crush on Ruby, and

she was one of his biggest fans.

The conveyor belt started moving. I craned my neck, even though Kyle was tall enough to see over the people in front of us. A familiar sound wailed from somewhere behind me. A violin?

I froze. A remembered strain of Ponte Vecchio's sidewalk music floated through my mind.

"I won't be able to stay." Kyle interrupted my thoughts. "I'm dropping you off and driving back."

"Tonight?"

He checked his watch. "This morning. It'll be morning by the time we get to the car and drive to Dana Point."

A handful of worn-out passengers from Flight 1902 were still waiting when my luggage finally tumbled out at the very end of the carousel, looking as tired and beat up as I felt.

We managed to get into Kyle's Porsche by 1:30. I'd suggested taking a taxi, but my son was adamant.

"Chill out. I've lost sleep for less worthy causes."

Deep down I was thankful, even felt special.

The Porsche was Kyle's high school graduation present. Nick had bought it at a police auction. Restoring the twelve-year-old convertible became father and son's grand project. Not that either one knew much about cars in general, or Porsches in particular. After many trips to the library and to used-parts dealers, the car began to look like new. Better than new. They decided on a rich shade of brown for the exterior and invested in some leather seats. By graduation, the Porsche was in mint condition. Kyle kept the car in top shape, even after all these years.

During the ride home, I told him about my strange encounter on Ponte Vecchio.

"And he had just vanished?"

"Pretty much. None of the other vendors acknowledged his earlier presence or his existence, for that matter. Very, very strange."

"What did the chart look like?" Kyle kept his eyes on the road.

"The way it used to before the computer era, I guess. I left it in my coat pocket. It's in one of the suitcases."

We traveled south on the 405. I always got excited when the San Diego Freeway merged with the Santa Ana. I told people that was when I could smell the brine. But that was a stretch of the imagination—the Pacific Ocean lay hills and canyons away. Then the ocean side of the freeway flattened, with fewer tall buildings and more tall trees. Even without daylight, I searched for a flash of blue water. I wouldn't see any. The ocean was as black as the sky. Still, it was one of my homecoming routines.

We pulled up to the security gate of my complex a little after 3:00 a.m. Kyle punched in the code, and the ornate wrought-iron gate slid open. The Porsche glided over the private road lined with palm trees and stopped in the guest parking.

I was still digging in my bag when my son used his key to unlock the front door of my town house. The moment I stepped across the threshold, a pungent stench hit my nostrils. I gagged. The smell of ammonia and cat feces was overpowering. The cat litter hadn't been changed in a very long time.

"Flash? Mommy's home. Here, kitty, kitty." I waited for a black shadow to dart into my arms. Nothing.

Kyle fanned himself with the weathered newspaper he'd picked up by my front door. "Phew, it's making me wanna puke. Why didn't you take Flash to Cat's Mirage?"

"Ruby offered to take care of her."

I opened the French doors leading to the back patio. Mail lay scattered across the thick glass dining room table. How odd. In the past, Ruby kept it organized every day.

"Mom, let's run through the place and make sure everything's okay. I've got to get going."

"Of course. I'm sorry."

Kyle followed me up the stairs.

We walked through the house and opened most of the windows. The smell of the filthy litter box improved only a little. "Everything looks fine. Better get going, and please take it easy, will you? I'd never forgive myself if something happened to you on your way back to Palm Springs."

"I'll call you." He hugged me and left.

I stood by the front door until his headlights came on. Then I wasted no time changing the litter box. I called my cat a few more times, and when I headed for the bedroom, something stroked my leg,

"Flash." I picked her up and rubbed my chin on her silky black head. "Are you mad at me for going away?" She cried while I carried her down to the kitchen. She felt so skinny. Could she be sick? Finally, she began to purr. Poverina, poor baby. I put her down and went into the laundry room for her dish. Both of Flash's food containers were empty, and her water bowl held only dust. I filled the water bowl and the dry-food container. What could have happened to keep Ruby from coming to the house? She wasn't the type of person to neglect a cherished pet on purpose. Maybe she called me at the hotel to prepare me for this? Nonsense. Why not call Kyle instead? He could have hired help.

I was tempted to phone Ruby and give her a piece of my mind. Knowing her, she must have found something very special to distract her. Her husband wouldn't appreciate a phone call at 3:45 a.m. I'd have to wait.

Still, I didn't like it. Idiot that I am, I wanted reassurance Ruby was okay.

The ringing of the phone woke me. A ribbon of sunshine draped across my hand when I picked up the receiver.

"Hello?"

"Mrs. York? Donatella York?"

I stifled a yawn and glanced at the alarm clock. 11:00 a.m.

No one called me Donatella. "Who is this?"

"I'm Lieutenant Devin, Orange County Sheriff's Department. I'm with the Homicide Division, ma'am."

"Homicide? Mio dio!"

"I need to speak with you at your earliest convenience."

"Excuse me. Did you say homicide?"

"Yes, ma'am. I need to speak to you about the Russell case."

"Ruby Russell?" I missed the rest of Devin's answer because I dropped the phone and lost the dial tone.

THREE

I needed to think about Ruby and about this cop, Devin. This homicide cop. He hadn't mentioned Ruby by name, but then again, I didn't know anyone else named Russell aside from Ruby and Tom. Barely awake and already under stress. Welcome home, all right. The quickest way to find out what was going on would be the direct approach. I picked up the phone and dialed Ruby's house.

Her recorded voice caught me off guard. "...but if you leave your phone number and a brief message..." I hung up. Pure torture. Listening to her voice and not knowing if she was dead or alive. I tried her cell, but it rang several times before going to a message that her mailbox was full.

The doorbell rang. My heart skipped a beat. Lieutenant Devin? So early? How did he get through the gate? Cops must have special passes. I fought my sense of dread and opened the door.

A boy, maybe five or six years old, stared at me. A new neighbor? I smiled, not sure what to do. Long time since I'd been around kids his age.

"Hi. You didn't get your paper." He handed me the Dana Point News.

I forgot my subscription was scheduled to restart delivery today. "Thank you." I took one end of the rolled-up paper, but he held on tight. Did he expect a tip?

"I live next door." His hair and complexion were unusually light, and he had the eyes of a child more grown up than he should have been. "My name is David." He let go of the paper. "Do you live here?"

I nodded, more puzzled than before.

"Where's the other lady?"

An uneasy feeling kept me from answering the child's

question. Footsteps sounded and a tall, dark-haired man walked up to the house and stood behind David, watching me.

"You must be Lieutenant Devin." I looked down. "I'll talk to you later, little boy." Calling him a little boy seemed to irk him; he frowned like older people did.

I invited the lieutenant in and closed the door on David's disappointed face.

"Thank you for seeing me on such short notice, Mrs. York."

"Yes, well, what is happening with my friend? I didn't quite comprehend what you were telling me—jet lag. I'm very concerned. I should have heard something, a phone call."

"I understand you've been out of the country."

"How do you know? Have you spoken to Ruby?" I still couldn't get myself to ask what I was dying to know: Is Ruby all right? "I got home from Italy last night—well, this morning. It's such a shock. I don't understand why Kyle didn't know. Kyle's my son."

He followed me into the living room and sat on the armchair across from me without hesitation. The lieutenant seemed to feel very comfortable. Too bad I didn't. I had expected a man in his position to be an endless source of information. Wrong. Seeing him so relaxed made me anxious. Why? I had nothing to hide, but growing up in Italy I always harbored great respect and a good dose of fear around people in uniforms. Devin wore civilian clothing.

"I'm sorry to be the one to break the news to you." His voice sounded only a tad above a whisper. Not intimidating at all. A learned expedient?

I waved my hand. "It's okay." I braced myself for what would come next.

"One of the neighbors interviewed after the accident suggested your name as the closest friend to the Russells."

"True. That's true." I took a breath. "Lieutenant, why

don't you get to the point? Tell me why...I mean, what has happened to Ruby?"

"Ruby—Mrs. Russell—you mean after she shot her husband?"

"What?" I opened and closed my mouth, the smoothness of his statement still piercing my eardrums. "No. No. Wait. You said...I thought...Ruby shot Tom? Ruby isn't dead?"

"Ruby?" He looked straight into my eyes and I noticed his.

Devin's eyes were gray, slightly almond shaped. Or maybe he cultivated an eternal squint to confuse people. Then again, my knowledge of detectives' habits was limited to ancient Columbo reruns on sleepless nights.

"Why did you assume Ruby to be the victim?" He tapped his fingers on the mini recorder he'd taken from his jacket pocket. The drumming sounded soft yet as precise as a metronome's rhythm. Time passed. The man knew how to wait.

I sat up straight and reached for my cup. I clamped my hands on the mug, head down, eyes closed. Ruby was alive. She shot her husband. Emotions rushed through my mind like debris in a hurricane. What was wrong with me? I couldn't decide if I felt relief or disappointment.

"Please, forgive me. This morning, when you called, I was sound asleep. I assumed..." I finally raised my eyes to him.

He relaxed against the back of the chair, returning my stare, his eyes as unreadable as before. "I apologize if I misled you. It happened in his office. He was cleaning the gun."

Tom had a gun? What for?

"He set it on the desk to answer the phone. Mrs. Russell—Ruby—picked it up, unaware the safety mechanism wasn't on. Supposedly, Mrs. Russell had never handled a firearm before. The gun went off, the bullet hit Mr. Russell in the back of the skull, and he died instantly. Mrs. Russell called 911, but there wasn't anything anyone could do. Any particular reason why you assumed it was Ruby who died, rather than her husband?"

The chart of a dead woman. "No." He couldn't be telling the whole story. It made no sense. Ruby would have called me. But then, she had. Was that what she needed to talk to me about that last night? Dear God, why didn't I try harder to get my call through to her?

"Mrs. York, there's nothing personal in my questions, only routine. I didn't mean to upset you." His voice sounded as monotone and calm as before.

It didn't matter, I was drowning in feelings of guilt. Guilt about what? Not being there for her? Not returning her phone call? Getting upset about her neglecting Flash? "When did it happen? Ruby left a message for me at the hotel just before I left Florence. Maybe she wanted to tell me about Tom." I expected more. I wanted Detective Devin to assure me I had nothing to blame myself for. I needed absolution.

"Four days ago—you and the Russells have been friends for a long time, right? I'd like your opinion of their relationship. Did they argue a lot? Were they happy?" The sound of his voice was getting under my skin. It forced me to pay closer attention than I preferred. And he knew it, I could sense it.

"Happy? What's your definition of happiness? Does it have a size? A color? A smell? Does it come in packages, by the pound or by the inch?" I talked like an opinionated, philosophical jerk, but I seemed unstoppable.

He ran his fingers over his forehead without disturbing the annoying perfection of the slicked-back style.

Could I do it? Run my fingers through his—Dio mio! What made me think about that? Something about this man pushed all my more regrettable buttons. I swallowed hard in my dry mouth.

He studied me, but I couldn't decipher a thing from his eyes. "The shooting has been ruled accidental."

Nick's death was accidental. And Ruby was with him when it happened. Just like she was with—

Stop it.

"But still...you're here."

"Just to make sure nothing has been overlooked, Mrs. York."

I nodded. He smiled, barely moving his lips. The smile spread, reaching his eyes, and suddenly Lieutenant Devin of Homicide became a real human being. A good-looking, well-dressed human being in a gorgeous charcoal suit with a perfect cut and constructed shoulders. French cuffs peeked out from his sleeves, and light gleamed from the small pyramid-shaped cuff links. Not what I expected a detective to wear. Columbo again.

How could I be so superficial? He'd just told me my best friend killed her husband, and I obsessed over his choice of threads? My glance went from his suit to his left hand. No wedding band. Probably in his late forties. I offered him coffee. He declined.

"I'll leave you one of my cards, just in case." His smile lingered.

I walked him to the door. My fingers clutched his business card like my sanity depended on that piece of printed paper.

LAWRENCE DEVIN. Larry? I liked the sound of his name.

He left and I ran upstairs, put on the pink sweater to match my dress, changed my shoes, grabbed my purse and the car keys and set forth to see Ruby. I tried to remember if I'd left gas in the car when I left for my Italian trip.

The little boy, David, stood by the rows of mailboxes. I kept the car on idle and went to check mine.

"Is that your mailbox?" His pale blue eyes looked puzzled.

"Of course it is." I rummaged for my key. "Why?"

"The other lady gets her mail in there too." He frowned, like a little old soldier standing guard. How odd.

"Oh, you must mean my friend Ruby. Yes, she did that while I was gone. Sort of. My mail and my cat." I sighed. Why was I talking to the little boy about Ruby's shortcomings?

I unlocked the box and looked inside: empty, except for a note from the mail carrier. Due to the volume, my mail waited for me at the post office, and if I wanted delivery to resume, I should call and request it. Great. Apparently Ruby stopped picking up the mail at about the same time she quit taking care of Flash. Answers. I needed answers. Good or bad. Anything would be better than wasting my time guessing and worrying. Why wasn't she picking up the phone? Ruby liked to talk, a lot. She called me at strange hours and from strange places. A lot more must be going on than what the detective shared. Could she be out of town? Where? I was determined to get answers, even if had to camp outside her door.

I eased into the northbound traffic flow on Golden Lantern. Dear God, I'd been gone less than a month and another ridge was already ravaged by construction, new dwellings sprouting on the hilltop. Kyle and I used to fantasize Laguna Niguel was the playground of the Green Giant. At night, he planted the seeds that grew into row after row of pink houses. Lately it looked as if he'd dumped the whole bucket of seeds all at once. So many houses. All looking alike. Reminded me of Lego blocks, as colorful and as generic. Just what we needed. More houses. Southern California was already overcrowded, according to my friends. It didn't matter to me. I loved the place in spite of the traffic, the high housing costs, the earthquakes and everything else that came with the territory.

Past Crown Valley, the scenery changed. No more pink houses. I approached the Nellie Gail Ranch. My stomach began to churn. Ruby moved here when she married Tom. The logical place for their fairytale wedding. Of course, the house didn't look exactly like this when they first bought it. With her background in fashion, Ruby had exquisite ways with colors, textures and spaces. Walls got removed, replaced and redesigned. Even the windows had to be "improved" to match the walls. Strangely, the kitchen was spared. Possibly because Ruby didn't care much about cooking, and Tom didn't have much luck when he tried to make remodeling suggestions. It all turned out fantastic. A big difference from Ruby's former place. Before marrying Tom, she lived in a garage turned cottage in Laguna Beach. Like Nick, she was an editor for the Orange County Register in Santa Ana.

Four years, and the thought of my husband's death still tore me apart.

I turned right and floored the gas pedal, my breathing short and sharp. Faster. Faster. I didn't want to feel the pain. I wanted to forget. Forget how I chose the clothes for his last dressing by the undertakers, careful not to let my tears mar his silk tie. Forget the touch of my fingers on his lifeless lips. Forget the coldness of the bed his body had warmed. Forget the empty garage where he used to keep his car.

Above all, I wanted to forget how he died.

Would it be the same for Ruby? No. It would be worse. It must be worse. She killed Tom. Accident or not, she was the cause. She'd have to live with that every day of her life.

Until death do us part. My wedding vows. Strange time to think about weddings and vows.

I drove along. Horses trotted on the bridle path. Young girls with long blond locks rode honey-colored mounts. California girls. California lifestyle. I made a left on Nellie Gail Road. Tears welled in my eyes. If only I could crawl somewhere and hide, the way cats did when they were sick. I couldn't. I was a grown woman on my way to comfort a friend. Better find a smile to put on my face.

The Russells' house—or, as Ruby called it, their French chateau, Orange County-style—had blue eaves and a three-car garage smack in the front. The ultimate multimillion-dollar tract mansion. I parked my car and checked my makeup in the rearview mirror. Habit. I pinched my cheeks for instant rosiness. Ready. The street was deserted, normal for this two-careers-one-mortgage neighborhood. All the drapes of the Russells' house were drawn closed, yet I had the feeling eyes from somewhere on the block watched my every move. I could only imagine the wagging tongues of the Home Owners Association. Poor Ruby. Maybe she avoided answering the phone because of that.

The doorbell echoed inside. I waited for what felt like an eternity. I rang again, my finger lingering on the button. I peeked through the etched glass panels of the front door. Darkness and silence seemed to fill the big house.

Devin's words echoed in my mind: "They were in his office. He was cleaning the gun. He set it on the desk to answer the phone."

I shivered and forced myself not to think about Tom. Who was I kidding? Dear God. Tom dead. Come on, Ruby, open the door. I wanted to scream her name and bang my fist on the glass door. Where could she be? After Nick's death, I went through loneliness and hopelessness. Dio mio. Ruby needed my help.

I tried her cell again, and again heard the same message about a full mailbox.

I walked back to the car, back stiff, knees weak from feeling stared at. I sat in the car, troubled. What to do? Four days ago, Ruby accidentally shot her husband. Tom was Ruby's only family. She loved him. I could testify to that in—testify? I fought the urge to go back to Ruby's door. I started the engine and headed toward the Dana Point post office to pick up my mail, only to find it closed. Why didn't I pay more attention? Look at my watch, step on the gas? Story of my life. What was that American saying? A day late and a dollar short? Yes, pretty much summed up my state of mind.

FOUR

That drive to Ruby's place had upset me more than I cared to admit. Why hadn't Ruby tried to reach me? Why wouldn't she return my calls? She needed someone who could listen, and help her to process Tom's death and the consequential problems.

I glanced at the setting sun, a shiny penny dipping into purple waters. Then I let the front door slam behind me and carried the groceries I'd stopped for on the way home into the kitchen. Another trip to the car should do it. Something I hated, a big drawback of the common garage. At least it wasn't raining.

When I dropped off the last bags, Flash eased down the stairs and paused for a moment. Her eyes followed me while I turned on the lights. She'd seemed jumpy since I returned from my trip to Italy.

"Hi, Flash. Look what I bought you." She walked over and rubbed against my leg. I ran my fingers over her arched back. A soft purr rewarded my stroking. After filling her dish and changing her water, I poured myself a glass of Chardonnay and sat on my favorite chair looking out onto the terrace. Since moving into this place, my life had been...peaceful, which was a creative way of avoiding the truth. In reality, my life consisted of an interrupted series of boring hours, days and months. In an attempt to broaden my circle of friends, a few years earlier I signed up for the Mission San Juan Docent program and, after the required hours of study, I graduated and went to work one day a week as a volunteer. It turned out to be more fun than anticipated. When I became a widow, I started to spend more time there, getting involved with the gift shop and helping make the little fragrant potpourri bags sold in the store. I should call to let them know I'm back. Tomorrow.

My thoughts returned to Ruby. Had she lost touch with reality four years after the car accident, the one that killed Nick and damaged her brain? What doctors thought was a concussion turned into blackouts and trouble forming short-term memories. She was doing great when I left.

Tired of watching Flash groom herself, I went into the kitchen and dialed Ruby's number. Five rings. I held my breath. No automated answer. Good. The phone kept on ringing. No voice mail, no Ruby. I dismissed the idea of calling her cell. She rarely checked the messages, so the mailbox was always full.

I sighed. Time to check my answering machine, something I hated even more than carrying bags of groceries from the car. After each absence I procrastinated as long as possible. Kyle told me I needed a digital service, but I preferred the old-fashioned style I'd had for so long. It did its job, and I knew how to use it.

Shades of red and purple from the setting sun bathed my bedroom walls. I liked my bedroom regardless of the time of day, but evenings like this made it even more special. I kicked off my shoes, made myself comfortable on the bed and, pad and pen in hand, hit the play button.

Someone wanted to sell me a subscription to the OC Register. I already subscribed to the newspaper. Hang-ups, a wrong number, my dentist's office reminding me of my appointment. Jet lag caught up with me, and I yawned. More hang-ups. Flash jumped onto the bed and snuggled up against my backside, purring. I listened to an offer for a free trip to Vegas.

Boring, boring—wait—

"Lella, guess what." Ruby's voice. A giggle. "I forgot, you aren't home. Silly me. I'll catch you later." Typical Ruby.

One of Nick's old friends passing through town invited me out to dinner. A week ago.

Dial tones.

I closed my eyes for a minute. A familiar voice woke me. A whisper. So close, was Ruby in the room? Speaking in my ear? I sat up, wide awake. The sound came from my answering machine. A chill stiffened the hair on the back of my neck, my heart pounding in my throat.

"I am in your house, scared to death, talking to your silly machine. Something strange is going on in your bedroom, Lella. Have you got a ghost?"

Why would she call my house phone from inside the house?

"I wish you had an upstairs exit." Fear in her voice. A shuffling sound. Was someone crawling on the carpet near the answering machine? The shuffle moved away. Why was she crawling? A creak on the tape sounded far away, like from the steps of my stairs? Ruby's muffled voice again. I couldn't understand what she said.

The chiming of the doorbell made me jump. I dropped the pad and pen, barely missing Flash. She bolted and hit the phone. It crashed to the floor. The doorbell rang again. I went downstairs, my legs shaky, turning on all the lights.

"Who is it?" I tried to control the quivering in my voice.

"I'm your neighbor. I'm looking for my little brother."

I opened the door.

No need to ask whose sister she was. In her early twenties, she had the same hair and fair complexion as the little boy, David. She tried to smile, but the worry in her hazel eyes shone through.

"I'm Lella York. I saw David earlier, in the afternoon."

"Oh, you've met him. Sorry, Audrey Bernard. I live next door. We moved in two weeks ago." She stood in the slice of light coming from my open door. The blue veins under the translucent skin of her slender neck pulsed. Long, straight hair hung around her young face. The dark, loose-fitting clothes she wore looked odd on her tall, thin body. Like borrowed rags or stolen garments. What was I thinking?

"You're David's sister? You're so adorable, just like him."

She shrugged then blushed. "I better go find him. He must have sneaked out while I was on the phone. It's getting late. Thank you, Mrs.York."

"Lella. Call me Lella." I closed the door. I had to go back to my answering machine. By now, my fear had morphed into uneasiness. I wanted to talk to someone, anyone. I wanted to be told everything would be okay. Should I call Kyle? How could I explain my state of mind to my son without upsetting and concerning him?

I went into the kitchen and dialed Ruby's number. The phone rang over and over. No answer. I didn't want to go upstairs.

In spite of my good intentions, I dialed Kyle's cell phone. "The mobile customer you have dialed—" I slammed the phone down. Where is everybody? Should I go out and talk to the strange young girl next door? Help her find her little brother, maybe? A glance at my bare feet changed my mind. Out of habit I'd left my shoes upstairs, same place as the answering machine with Ruby's message.

Lawrence Devin's name popped into my mind. Larry. I couldn't possibly call him this late. He probably wasn't at the office anyway. I started up the stairs.

Flash sat on the top landing, licking her front paw. Lucky cat. She didn't have a worry in the world. She stretched and followed me down the hall. Feeling like a complete idiot, I checked the guest room and even looked in the closet. Thank God the shutters were closed. I didn't want the neighbors to see what I was doing.

What was I doing? Becoming paranoid? I checked the guest bathroom also. The door seemed stuck. I bumped it open with my hip. I went to the corner cabinet to get a new roll of toilet paper to replace the empty one. The cold carpet against my bare soles gave me chills. I stared at the toilet paper. It wasn't the brand I usually bought. I preferred the two-ply kind, well worth the extra pennies. This was single ply. Not a big deal, just strange. Did Kyle buy toilet paper thinking we didn't have any? Did Ruby?

I bent down to check the carpet; damp. "Flash, did you do this?" On my hands and knees, I reached for her. She bolted back and disappeared. I didn't smell cat urine. What happened here? Too tired to clean floors, I retreated into my bedroom, where another surprise awaited. A soft buzz came from my night table. Correction, from under my night table, where the telephone had landed on top of the answering machine. It was the sound of the machine whirring. All the messages had been erased.

"Flash? Where are you hiding?" I put the telephone back on the night table. "Well, I guess one of my problems is solved." I couldn't listen to Ruby's message since it was erased. No sense dwelling on it. Who was I kidding? The night chill descended over South Orange County while I sat against the pillow, hypnotized by my own spell.

A noise came from under my bed. There was Flash, all curled up. "Flash, you big coward." She opened one eye to look at me then closed it again and went back to sleep.

Great.

Maybe a sleeping pill would help.

I undressed, put on my nightgown and my robe and went into the bathroom to remove my makeup.

On my way to the closet, I picked up the handbag I'd left on the floor. Lawrence Devin's business card fell out.

The sign I'd been waiting for. I knew it. I didn't care if it was almost midnight. I dialed the number on his card. A woman answered the phone.

"Can I speak to Lieutenant Devin, please?"

"Devin?" She paused. "Just a moment."

I waited, trying to come up with something to say. Why was I calling this man?

My hands sweated, yet chills ran through my body. I can hang up. I didn't say who I am.

"I'm sorry, ma'am. Lieutenant Devin is on vacation. Would you like to speak to someone else?"

"What?" I stared at the white card in my hand, the printed words dancing in slow motion. "Are you sure? Never mind. It's not a big deal." I didn't wait for an answer. I put down the phone. My mind whirled. When had he gone on vacation? He'd just interviewed me this morning. Had he wrapped up the case so fast? And if so, what of Ruby? If he'd already made up his mind about her, why would he go through that questions-and-answers charade with me? What could he gain from it? He didn't ask me to sign anything. He wasn't threatening. On the contrary, he was charming and handsome. Stop it. I was becoming much too paranoid. I tore the business card into shreds then turned off the light.

FIVE

Morning light tortured my headache and my eyelids weighed a ton—each. Even a cup of my favorite brew failed to improve my disposition. I picked up the newspaper from the front door and decided it was time to talk to Ruby face to face. Flash came from the laundry room, sat by the kitchen door and licked her paws. She watched me dial Ruby's number.

Two rings and a chime, then a voice informed me that the number I had dialed was no longer in service.

I must have dialed the wrong number. Carefully, I redialed. Same recording. I slammed the phone down. Flash interrupted her routine, gave me a disdainful glance and disappeared under the living-room couch. I could blame Ruby for only part of my lousy state of mind. Lieutenant Devin had joined the ranks of the people I'd like to have a word or two with.

Time to get dressed. The empty space in my walk-in closet reminded me I had to unpack my suitcase, which in turn reminded me Kyle hadn't called since he dropped me off.

God, I looked awful. I wasn't in any mood for makeup, either. I tied a scarf over my hair to hide the few gray roots playing peekaboo on my head, grabbed my movie-star-incognito dark glasses and left.

At the security gate, I crossed paths with the mail carrier. "Hi, Juliet." I waved my mail slip from my car window.

Juliet shielded her eyes from the sun and walked over. "Nice to have you back, Mrs. York. Sorry about your mail. I didn't have much choice. The mailbox was full."

"Don't apologize. I understand."

"That's good. Your friend should learn from you."

"My friend?"

"The one who's been taking care of your mail and, I guess, your house."

"Oh, you mean Ruby. What has she been up to?"

"She was here yesterday and got very upset when I told her your mail had to be picked up at the post office."

"Yesterday?"

"Yes. Is there something wrong?"

"No. No. I've got to go. Ciao."

Ruby was here yesterday? Why didn't she come over to the house? She must have felt terrible when she found out the post office stopped delivering my mail. I bet she was ringing my doorbell while I was ringing hers. I'd drive to her house first and tell her about her phone being out of order. Maybe she didn't pay the bill. Tom always took care of their finances. Poor Ruby. What would become of her now?

Her husband had to have a substantial trust fund set up for her, and life insurance. Like Nick did. Where would I have been without Nick's insurance after his death?

I wasn't going to think about him. Fifteen minutes later the blue eaves of the Russells' house came into view, and I parked at the curb. Eaves weren't the only blue thing I noticed. Right on the sad-looking front lawn, next to the wilting miniature roses, there was a blue and white realty sign. FOR SALE. What? I got out of my car and marched to the front door.

I rang the bell a dozen times. Each time I left my finger on the button longer and longer. No answer.

Discouraged, and a little angry, I walked down the front path. The neighbor across the street, armed with a straw hat, gloves and gardening tools, appeared absorbed in her work. Or was she?

Mrs. Snoopy, Ruby called her.

"Hell, I know there's one in every neighborhood," Ruby used to say, "but must she live across the street from me?"

I walked over. "Hi there. I'm Lella York, Ruby's friend."

"How are you? We met at the Russells' housewarming party, remember? Poor Tom. What a terrible way to go." She stopped to take a breath.

I nodded.

"Of course, I had the feeling something wasn't right, especially after the incident with the Jeep."

"What incident?"

"You don't know? Come to think of it, I haven't seen you around lately. Not before yesterday." She stopped.

So she had been keeping an eye on the house.

"I was out of the country on vacation."

She shrugged. "Never could understand why a little person like her would drive that big car in the first place. Anyhow, they'd just gotten one of those gadgets. You push a button on your garage opener and all your lights come on or go out. In the house, I mean."

I hoped I looked fascinated by her story.

"Sears installed it two weeks ago. The night before she killed—I mean, before the accidental shooting, she got home very late. I happened to be walking Gigi, my French poodle. Right when she came around the curb, Ruby, I mean, must have pushed the wrong button because the house went completely dark." Mrs. Snoopy removed her wide-brimmed hat and paused. I was impatient for her to get back to the story. She seemed to enjoy herself too much.

I nodded and sighed. It must have been what she wanted to see, because she resumed her storytelling.

"Ruby finally managed to get the garage door open. I bet she pressed every button on the remote. I could see her shaking it. And then, as the garage door closed, a crash reverberated and the house went dark again. Tom came out the front door in his slippers and robe, looking puzzled. He asked me what had happened. Can you imagine?" She laughed a short, forced laugh. "It turned out Ruby pushed more than one wrong button. She closed the garage door and at the same time, the back gate of the Jeep swung open. I'm not sure how she did it, but the car door got jammed into the garage door and they couldn't move one without damaging the other. Tom finally managed to get the garage closed, but I bet the Jeep is still that way, stuck to the garage door."

"Are you saying Ruby's Jeep is in the garage and can't be moved?"

"I'm sure Tom would have taken care of it if he hadn't been killed. And you know how Ruby is."

Sure, Ruby still got confused sometimes, but she wasn't scatterbrained like this woman implied.

"By the way, do you know where Ruby is? I've been trying to reach her."

"No. I can't say I do. Then again, I'm not spending my time checking on the neighbors."

Right!

"This morning a realtor came to put up the FOR SALE sign."

I nodded. "I imagine the police questioned you."

"Oh, yes, they did. I don't know what for. They ruled Tom's death an accident. Though, by all accounts, Ruby's running around like nothing happened." She avoided my eyes.

"Did you speak to Lieutenant Devin?"

"Who?"

"Never mind. I'd better get going. If you see Ruby, can you tell her I've been trying to get in touch?"

"Sure. Have you tried calling her?"

"Her phone seems to be out of order."

"It is?"

"I'll let you get back to your garden. Goodbye."

When I got to my car, I jotted down the real estate company's phone number. I watched Mrs. Snoopy hurrying inside. Dying to share the latest gossip with the rest of her garden club? I didn't even remember her name.

Where could Ruby be? Sure, she didn't try to control her impulsive nature. However, this was way past that. This was—I didn't want to fill in the blanks, didn't want to face the impending truth. Was she really losing it? Time to stop that kind of nonsense and pay attention to my driving. Especially to the flickering red light, the one telling me my car was running on fumes. I needed to focus on finding a gas station and then getting myself to the post office. Locating Ruby would have to wait.

"Okay, Flash, you can stop biting my ankle. I know you're hungry. So am I, and I'm moving as fast as I can."

My cat had been hanging on my leg from the minute I came through the front door. She let go when the bowl of dry food was placed on the kitchen floor.

I made myself a peanut butter sandwich, the crunchy kind. Standing in the middle of the kitchen, munching, I glanced at the mail piled on the dining room table. I'd have to go through that soon. What a nuisance.

The phone rang.

"Hello?"

"Mrs. York?"

"Speaking." I tried to swallow the big chunk of bread filling my mouth.

"Mrs. York, this is Lawrence Devin. My office called. I'm told you tried to reach me last night. Did you need to speak to me?"

"Your office said you were on vacation." I forced myself to speak without resentment. "Weren't you working on Tom Russell's death?"

"That death was ruled accidental. Unless you have something to add."

"No. I just wondered about the timing." The timing, sure.

"I went on vacation right after I filed the paperwork clearing Mrs. Russell of any wrongdoing. If you need to tell me something, though, I'm available. Any time."

He sounded honest enough. I didn't know what to say. Why was I so tongue-tied?

"I'm calling from my car. I'll be back in a week and I'd like to have dinner with you if you're interested."

My tongue stuck to the peanut butter on the roof of my mouth. My brain functioned fine. His stormy gray eyes and the way his buns filled his pants came to mind. This was the best offer I'd had in months. Months? Years.

"Why don't you call me when you get back and we'll set up a time?" Ask for his phone number, stupid. Caller ID showed number unavailable.

"Good. I'll talk to you then. Bye." Click.

I stood there, holding the phone, my brain in shock. Then I danced an impromptu tarantella around the spotless kitchen and ended up kicking Flash's bowl. Poor baby. She was probably wondering what had gotten into me. What if it was a trick? Maybe he was still searching for information regarding Tom's death. Whatever. Better than staying around the house, alone.

I sat at the dining-room table, a brown paper bag next to me to recycle the junk mail, with a box for the rest.

The crystal chandelier cast a circle of light around me. It was a quiet night for a Friday. No pool parties.

On top of the pile sat a postcard with a smiling dog brushing his teeth. From my dentist. My appointment was next week.

Bank statement. Must balance my checking account. Black out the account numbers. Trash.

A letter in Ruby's handwriting. The envelope came from her stationery, but it looked beat up, crumpled. I studied my address. She wrote the wrong zip code. She'd scratched it out and written the right one underneath it. Ruby was always fussy about her correspondence. It surprised me she hadn't replaced the envelope with a new one. She mailed the letter after I'd gotten home. Fear resurfaced. I tore the envelope open, pulled out the white paper and two keys fell onto the table. My house and mailbox keys. The paper was blank, except for the two Rs interlaced at the top, like a Rolls Royce logo.

I kept staring, confused. What did it mean? The glow from the chandelier reflected on the keys. They shone like gold. Why mail the keys? Why not give them to me in person? Was she avoiding me? We'd had lunch the day before my trip; she drove me to the airport and everything was fine. This blank letter, the keys—the whole thing felt like a goodbye of some sort.

I got up and went to pour myself some Chardonnay. Changed my mind, settled on some bottled water and went back to the mail. I didn't understand any of this. Better to finish with the mail.

An invitation to a gallery opening. Keep or trash? Think about it.

Advertisements. End-of-the-month clearance. Bills.

A refund check from my broker. Good.

A letter from Mission San Juan Capistrano reminding me of the volunteers' planning meeting for the Return of The Swallows on March nineteenth.

That was tomorrow. I groaned. I had to be there.

I was tired. I could watch the news upstairs and go to sleep. The light on the answering machine told me I had a message.

"Hi, Mom, I may be able to stop by tomorrow or the day after. Not sure yet. I'll let you know. Ciao." Kyle's voice did my heart good. First Lawrence Devin, now Kyle. Only one not accounted for. Ruby.

SIX

Time spent at the mission felt more like a reward than work. A time for renewal. The twelve of us regulars made it a habit to leave our personal agendas outside the massive gate of the historical landmark. While the new church built in the '80s to replace the one destroyed by the 1812 earthquake was an architectural masterpiece, we preferred to meet in the old section of the mission to discuss how to divide our duties for the day. We knew no swallow would darken the sky on March nineteenth, or any other day, at least not on the way to the mission, but tradition must be carried on and the town of San Juan Capistrano had three days of festivities planned around the event that celebrated the return of the cliff swallows from Argentina. My assignment was to answer the phones. Many calls came in from overseas and started very early in the morning. No one forced us to wear a costume, but we all did it. Such a fun practice. I wore my black suede skirt with matching fringed vest and my red silk blouse from Florence, and I tied the whole look together with my gaucho hat. That and my new Italian boots. The thought of the boots brought back images of the astrologer and, of course, Ruby.

Sabrina, one of the volunteers who worked at the gift shop, noticed my mood change. "Is something wrong?"

I shook my head. "I haven't seen Ruby since I got back, so I'm a little concerned."

"Poor thing. I read about her husband. They were married such a short time. It's too bad. Maybe she's staying under the radar for a while, to avoid the gossip."

"Gossip? About what? I wish I could have been there for her. I was in Italy when it happened. Poor Ruby—she called, but the phone service overseas is very different. We didn't connect."

"That's right. Bad things tend to happen to Ruby when you are gone. Strange coincidence. No reflection on you, of course. We know it was an accident. Still, Tom is gone and so is your husband. Both accidental deaths, and Ruby goes about her life, unscathed."

What an unkind comment. I kept my mouth shut, nodded my head and went back to talking about the phones. Should have left my personal life outside the gate as usual. Sabrina seemed to take the hint and resumed stuffing envelopes to solicit donations with a bit more eagerness.

California's missions have always fascinated me, and I read everything I could find on the subject. Of all the ones I'd visited, Mission San Juan Capistrano was my favorite. After all, they'd named the mission, and later the town, after an Italian saint, San Giovanni da Capestrano. Loved the Italian connection; it made me proud. This place oozed history and stories. After most of the day spent at the mission and in no mood to cook, instead of going straight home I headed toward the grocery store to pick up some takeout from the deli counter.

At the traffic light, waiting to turn left, I glanced at the Old Dana Point Cafe courtyard. Memories ambushed me. Damn you, Sabrina, you had to bring up Nick's death. The place looked sad and deserted. Stacks of patio chairs sat next to the closed red and white umbrellas. Even the chattering fountain had hushed. A few dead leaves dangled from the naked trees. Rumors had been circulating the place had been sold to a commercial developer, and snazzy condos would replace the existing buildings. Just what we needed, more cramped residences and more people.

Six years ago the settings were quite different. Six years can be swift or endless. Six years ago I met Ruby for the first time.

A few weeks after Kyle graduated from high school, Nick and I drove south, to Dana Point, looking at open houses. After spending Sunday afternoon in and out of homes for sale, we felt hot and tired. Nick decided to stop for a drink.

Coming into the dark from the outside brightness, I squinted, embraced the coolness of the place and heard music. No, not just music—jazz.

We stood in a poorly lit hall. Photos of musicians covered the walls. Where were we?

Nick put his arm around my waist and coaxed me on. We walked under an arch and into the main room.

We'd come in through the back entrance of the Old Dana Point Cafe and found ourselves next to the small wooden stage where a jazz quartet performed. The players seemed old. Plenty of wrinkles, not much hair. The face of the pianist looked weathered beyond repair, but the hands flying across the keyboard possessed the passion of youth.

The place was packed, and we climbed onto barstools. A musty smell came from the well-stocked bar.

Nick leaned over. "What would you like?"

"Sparkling water with lemon." I had to shout for him to hear me. "I'm going to the ladies' room." I slid off the stool. Applause erupted. The musicians bowed and put down their instruments. I didn't know places like this existed in Orange County. It reminded me of old movie scenes, when ladies wore hats and men removed theirs.

A few hours here and you could forget the heat just outside the massive door or the roar of the surf on Doheny Beach a hundred yards away. Perhaps Dana Point wasn't a bad place to live.

I had to fight my way back from the ladies' room, through the crowded main room. Head tilted, Nick was caught up in conversation with a dark-haired woman. From where I stood, I could only see her back. She was short, like me, and seemed to be stretching on her toes, despite her stiletto heels. Trying to get as close as possible to Nick's face?

Her scanty dark blue dress, with a scalloped hem, showed off the rich tan of her shapely legs. Short, curly hair gave her the look of an Italian cherub. Was her hand resting on my husband's thigh? I couldn't tell. I quickened my pace. He still hadn't noticed me. His face had that why-am-I-enjoying-this-when-I-shouldn't look.

"Hi." My voice a little louder than I'd meant it to be. I stood mere inches from the woman's derriere.

Nick jumped. I couldn't tell if her hand slid off his leg or the edge of the stool.

"Honey." His voice strained. "This is Ruby Alexander. She works at the newspaper. My wife, Lella."

When Ruby turned around, her bust line rose about three inches and somehow stayed there. She smiled. Her lips were red—the brightest, glossiest red I'd ever seen.

I offered my hand. "Ruby Alexander—the fashion editor?"

Her eyes lit up. They were dark and liquid, but something else set them apart. Ruby's eyes were—voracious. The word slammed into my mind like a wrecking ball. And yet it was the right word, for an insatiable hunger seemed to come from within her. Hunger for what? Or whom?

She took my hand in hers. "You read the fashion page?"

"Every Friday." I did.

She nodded.

Someone pushed a stemmed glass filled with clear, straw-colored liquid toward Ruby. "Oh, thank you, Charlie." She picked up the wine and sampled it. "Chimney Rock." She turned toward the bar and lifted the glass to the tall bartender. He winked.

"Do you come here often?" I asked.

"Any chance I get, especially on Sunday. I simply looove jazz."

She uttered the word "love" with a little gasp, like an orgasmic cry. Everything about Ruby seemed spontaneous. She appeared to inhale life by big gulps. Against my better judgment, I found myself liking her.

Nick cleared his throat. I glanced at him. Twenty-three

years of sharing the seesaws of life told me he was ready to
leave.

Ruby offered to show me around the area in the coming
weeks. I accepted and soon found myself fascinated by this
woman. I pursued her friendship even when instinct warned
me not to. Ruby kept her word. We toured open houses and
model homes. With Kyle close to leaving home for college,
Nick and I had to decide if we wanted to move south or stay
put. Ruby lived in Laguna Beach and, unlike Nick, she didn't
commute and worked mostly at home. We met for late
lunches. She introduced me to California's new generation
of wines. Ruby's true passions? Wine and jazz.

At forty-five, she'd been married and divorced three
times, and she still dreamed of Prince Charming driving a
white Ferrari Testarossa. While waiting for the prince, she
kept herself busy—often with more than one man.

"Hell, use it or lose it." She didn't have to explain what
"it" was. Oddly enough, she didn't discuss any lover in
particular, and I never met any of them.

Ruby worshipped the sun. After our family settled into
our new home, I spent many afternoons at the beach with
her. I wore a big hat; she soaked in the rays. Her nose had
the redness of overexposed skin, but instead of detracting
from her looks, it seemed to fit her all-or- nothing attitude.

Did opposites really attract? It appeared that way. I
often thought of Ruby as the Hollywood version of plain old
me.

Ruby fascinated Kyle too. He hung around her place on
his time off—willing to run errands, or wash her car. Puppy
love?

On a dare, she used him for a fashion spread. We all
gathered around the kitchen table that Friday morning,
opened the fashion page and shrieked with excitement. Kyle,
my baby, shone on the glossy sheet. A golden boy against the
endless cobalt sky. Soon the phone was ringing, and the next
thing I knew, he was a rising star. Goodbye, college.

During our first spring in Dana Point, things began to go wrong. My mother became very ill, and Kyle got entangled with a much older but still famous movie star, a married woman who was breaking his heart. I felt helpless; why couldn't I stop my loved ones from suffering?

On a late summer morning, Ruby called while Nick finished his second cup of coffee. Her car wouldn't start, and she had an important meeting at the paper. Could Nick give her a ride?

He did, and soon they were carpooling several times a week. Their return route grew longer and longer. Toward the end, Nick sometimes missed dinner altogether. Was I too distracted by my family problems to notice the signs? Perhaps I refused to see them. Wasn't denial the ultimate placebo?

Some nights the phone rang, and I was afraid to pick it up. What would it be this time? My dying mother? Kyle on the brink of suicide? Or another of Nick's late, late business meetings?

When Mother was diagnosed with cancer, I packed my bag and flew to Italy.

I was there when it happened.

Kyle called. His father was dead, killed in a car accident.

"Please, Mom. Come home."

I don't remember what I did or said. I don't remember getting to the airport or even the flight home. When I arrived at LAX I was still in denial. Somebody was playing tricks on me. Nick dead? Impossible. He wouldn't do that to me.

Kyle picked me up in Nick's car. Nick's car?

I waited until we reached the freeway to ask.

"Mother." His voice more like a whimper. I noticed how pale he was—and thin too. That woman he got involved with was destroying him.

"...driving her car, and..."

"Wait! Whose car?"

"Mother, haven't you been listening?"

I shrugged.

"Dad was driving Ruby's car. The brakes failed on the way down Ortega Highway, a mile or so above San Juan Hot Springs. You know—the same damn spot...." He shook his head.

Every resident of South Orange County knew someone who'd had a close call in that same damn spot.

"What was your father doing on Ortega Highway in Ruby's car?" My voice sounded shrill. I had to blame someone. I had to unleash the rage inside me. I needed a scapegoat.

"What difference does it make? When Ruby comes out of the coma...if she comes out of it, you can ask her."

I cried. Nick was dead. It wasn't fair. I needed him. I loved him. It was my fault. I should have been there. How could I go on without him? I wasn't strong enough.

Kyle kept his head and shoulders upright. He may have been hurting more than I was, but he wasn't giving up.

"Why, God? Why, Nick?" I choked on my questions.

Kyle drove the rest of the way in silence.

SEVEN

The phone rang as I ran up the stairs. I answered it in my bedroom.

"Hello."

"You sound breathless."

I frowned. "Who is this?"

"Larry." He must have misunderstood my silence. "Lieutenant Lawrence Devin of Homicide, ma'am." He spoke in a surprising imitation of the Dragnet monotone. Then he laughed a low, intimate laugh.

"I thought you were going to call in a week."

"I'm calling now. How about dinner?"

Did he want to talk about the case or was this a social call? Did I even care? I kicked off my sandals "When?"

"Tonight."

I unfastened my jeans. "Tonight?" Stepped out of them.

"I drove all the way back from Parker, Arizona, and to be honest, the idea of my dark, empty house doesn't seem very appealing. I'm hungry, so if you haven't eaten, I'd like to take you to dinner."

I unbuttoned my blouse. "Where are you?"

"At your gate." That laughter again. "Only kidding—but not too far."

My bra came off, and then my panties. "Give me thirty minutes. How should I dress?" Was that really my voice? God, I sounded so self-assured I almost believed it.

He hesitated. "Something pink?"

I laughed at his answer. Typical male. I'd meant if I should be casual or formal.

"Pink? Maybe. See you soon." Two minutes later I had the water running in the bathtub.

From where we sat at Cannons restaurant, the lights of the

boats out at sea looked like fireflies on a sultry summer night. Below us, spotlights flooded The Pilgrim's main mast. The ship was a perfect replica of the vessel that brought Richard Henry Dana into the harbor in 1834. Dana Point had been named after him. We were looking at the same waters, from the same cliffs.

"You weren't very hungry, were you?" Larry asked.

I turned away from the harbor.

"Don't talk much either." His fingers brushed mine.

The busboy poured the coffee then left.

"We—I love this place. I haven't been here in a while." I took a breath and then stirred my coffee, avoiding his gaze. I'd mentioned Nick at the beginning of the meal, which made it hard not to think about him.

"It's a great spot."

"I like the food." I stopped just short of confessing he was my first date in over two years, and I worried I'd say or do something wrong. He leaned toward me. The flickering candle threw his face into shadow. His lashes flirted with his tanned cheeks every time he blinked, and he stared at me. The warmth of his hand covered mine. I couldn't think, couldn't move.

The busboy came back to our table. "More coffee?"

I pulled away and turned my head. I stared at our reflections on the glass wall. We looked joined, as one. I sat back, and we were two again. He didn't let go of my hand. I breathed quietly. Could he hear the racket my heart made beneath the shimmering of my pink silk blouse?

"How was fishing?"

He blinked in response. "Fishing?"

We looked at each other. I nodded, aware my question killed the mood.

"Fishing—of course—fishing." He drummed his fingers on the table. I waited. The bill came. He pulled out his wallet and put down a credit card. "We never made it out of Parker."

"We?" I immediately hated that I needed to know who the other half of that equation was.

"My buddy and I. Steve is a detective with the Parker Police Department. We go back a long way. He was with the Orange County office. Anyhow, I got there yesterday morning. We loaded his Bronco and were ready to take off when they called him in. A drowning case just below the dam. Some kids found the body. I wasn't sure this was the kind of conversation you would have enjoyed with your meal."

"I'm fascinated. Was it an accident?"

He shrugged. "Nah. Apparent suicide. She left a note."

"A woman?"

"Some local. The family has a history of mental instability. Steve knew them. Her brother is in a mental institution. Sad case. We decided to postpone the trip. I drove home. He went to the office to fill out the transfer papers."

"Transfer papers?"

"The body—pardon me, the victim had to be taken to Tucson for the autopsy. How did we get on this subject?" He shook his head. "Let's go." He stood and helped me from my chair.

Outside, a dark sky and a mild night set the tone. We paced, waiting for the skinny teenager to bring Larry's Mercedes around. I couldn't hear or see the ocean from Cannons parking lot, but I breathed in the brine.

Larry's profile was an interesting series of strong lines and precise angles. A strand of hair fell onto his forehead. I reached to brush it back but caught myself. He seemed familiar with the streets. I sensed he studied me from the corner of his eye as much as I studied him.

The teen brought the car around.

"Nice car."

"Thanks."

"New?"

"Yes."

How could he afford this kind of car on a detective's salary?

"You're wondering how I could afford it."

I nodded, heat rushing to my face as we got in.

"I won the lottery."

What? I couldn't see his eyes and his voice wasn't giving me any clue. Was he joking?

I laughed. The tension was getting to me.

"What's so funny?" He looked straight ahead.

I searched for an intelligent reply but couldn't think of anything to say while the sound of my laughter filled the car.

"Twice a week, every Saturday and Wednesday, someone wins the state lottery. Not always the grand prize, but there are other winners."

"Larry, you don't look or act nouveau riche. It's as if you were born into it." When did he pull to the side of the road and stop the car?

The way he looked at me had me gulping for air. Bathed in the amber glow of the dashboard, his eyes held on to mine. Without a word he reached across me and touched something on the car door. My seat hummed and began to recline. He leaned, pressing my shoulders against the soft leather of the seat, his lips on mine, his tongue probing my mouth. My head felt empty, as if a giant vacuum had sucked out my brain, and, with it, all my self-control. Through the light fabric of his shirt, the heat of his body warmed my breasts. And slowly, without logic, I relaxed, wanting more. He pulled me tighter against him, cupped my face with his free hand. His thumb stroked my neck, the tip of his tongue in my ear, circling, teasing.

"Hmm." The sound escaped from the back of my throat. A whispery, husky response to his kiss. That was all I could get from my frozen brain while my body burned. My hands were on his shoulders, pulling him closer, holding on to him.

The heart is an organ of fire. The line from Ondaatje's

The English Patient crossed my mind. Blood coursed through my body, and we were as close to spontaneous combustion as humanly possible.

"Lella," he whispered, his mouth close to the nape of my neck, his breath putting goose bumps all over my body. "Lella." A little louder. Only my name. How long had it been since a man spoke my name in the darkness of a car? I couldn't handle the intensity. I pushed him away. He resisted at first then relaxed back against his seat and tucked his shirt in. I lay there a moment staring up at him. I sighed and raised my seat up.

The engine must have been idling the whole time, because he simply shifted gears and the car began to move.

We drove in silence. A silence void of uneasiness. I've always been amazed by the different meanings of silence. It could be emotionally charged or empty silence—nothing to say. Angry silence—after a fight. Anyway, it was never just silence.

My body quivered, still under the spell. He held the steering wheel with his left hand. His right one cupped my knee. What would happen next? Should I ask him in for a nightcap? Or kiss him good night before getting out of the car? This was idiotic. I had regressed into puberty. Because of a kiss? Well, not just any kiss. That kiss was a promise, a beginning. We reached my gate. I clicked the control and the gate swung open. Larry kept his eyes straight ahead and his hand on my knee. I had to decide how to end the evening. Problem was, I didn't want it to end.

Even with the lights on, the underground garage wasn't very bright. He slowed down when we reached the main entrance; the beam from the Mercedes' headlights shined on rows of parked cars. I recognized the familiar shape of the car sitting on the stall next to mine. A brown Porsche.

Kyle's car.

Dilemma resolved. The instant Larry stopped the car, I jumped out. With a quick "I'll call you, ciao," I strolled down the walkway. If he said something. I didn't hear him. The only sound came from my high heels clicking on the stones of the path leading to my front door. All the windows of my town house were dark. No lights. Strange. I unlocked the front door and stepped in. "Hello. Anybody here?" Silence. Where was Kyle? He couldn't have seen me in the car with Larry. What a relief. We'd never talked about the possibility of future dates. A conversation I dreaded.

Something brushed my ankle. I jumped back, startled.

"Meow." I turned on the light. "Flash, you scared me to death. Is Kyle here?" Smart Lella. A talking cat, right? I checked every room. Nothing, but his car was in the garage. Kyle must have gone out with friends. I could have asked Larry in after all.

Upstairs in my room, I undressed. That kiss did a number on me, couldn't get it off my mind. Oh God, I didn't know Larry's phone number. Except for the police department, and he was technically still on vacation.

In the middle of my bathroom I stood, staring at myself in the mirror. Nuda come un verme. "Naked as a worm," my mother used to say. I cupped my hands under my breasts and pushed up. Hmm, much better. I could understand why women got breast implants and face lifts. Understand or justify? Maybe one of those Wonderbras would help. Get a grip, Lella. It was just a kiss. I put on my nightgown, got under the covers and turned off the light.

EIGHT

When I was a little girl, my mother used to braid my long, straight hair into tight, intertwining strands. She pulled it back so tightly that from the front, it looked as if I had no hair. One scorching summer afternoon, Mother filled a wooden tub with cool water and let me play in it. An exciting new experience for me. My braids came untied. My hair fell on my shoulders and all the way to my waist. It was as if the hair took on a life of its own. My hair. Part of me, yet out of my control. Like my emotions. For most of my life I'd kept them tucked away, nicely intertwined in the hidden places of my soul. From the outside it appeared as if I had no feelings. It simplified my life. I could handle leaving home for a new country, loving Nick the way he liked it. His perfect little wife. A reflection of his expectations. A product of his wants.

Last night's kiss untied my emotions like I had been dipped into a cauldron of desire. I was afraid to look at myself in the mirror, afraid all that mass of passion showed on my face. It was that concern about my feelings seeping through that kept me tucked in my bed instead of running to welcome Kyle when I heard the front door open last night.

This morning the sun filtered through the drapes, creating new shadows on my old, familiar bedroom furniture. I looked at myself in the mirror before going to say hello to Kyle. I'd had vivid dreams all night, mainly starring Larry Devin. I wanted to make sure I didn't look too disheveled. Apparently all the changes took place in my head, since the face in the mirror looked just the same. Now I felt old and full of doubts. The more I studied myself, the more depressed I became. My nightgown looked frumpy and out of style. Just like my hair, and my lingerie, and—enough.

Flash was giving me a look. She didn't care about my internal crisis. She wanted breakfast.

I put on my slippers and quietly went downstairs. The open door of the guest room brought me to a halt. I nearly stepped on Flash. She jumped and ran with a loud meow. I peeked in. The bed hadn't been touched. Everything seemed just like the night before. Where was Kyle? Maybe he left his stuff downstairs and ran out to join his friends? I couldn't see a trace of Kyle ever being in the house. I knew I saw his car in the parking garage last night. I was absolutely certain. Flash's scratching at my ankles started to annoy me. Not a good sign. I fed her while the coffee brewed. I had just retrieved the daily newspaper from the front door when the phone rang. I hesitated, not recognizing the local number. Could it be Larry?

It was Sabrina, from the mission. "Oh, Lella, I'm sorry."

"Sorry about what?" I fought to control the stress level in my voice.

"Haven't you heard about Ruby? It was on the news. Her house burned down last night."

Not about Kyle. Relief and guilt battled for control. "Is Ruby okay?"

"I'm guessing so. The news reported the estimated damaged to the house, but they never mentioned anyone dying. I got the short version while I watched Good Morning America. You know how they break for brief local news. I thought you knew."

"I didn't read the paper yet."

"I doubt it made the paper, since it happened quite late last night."

"Maybe I should get over there. Thanks, Sabrina. Got to go." I hung up on her before she could say another word.

I ran upstairs, got dressed and had almost made it out the door when the phone rang again. "Good Morning, Lella." Larry.

With all the opening lines I had been rehearsing, I

found myself tongue-tied again.

"Lella? Are you okay?" He sounded concerned, but not too concerned.

"I can't talk to you. Got to run." I hung up while cursing myself and my lack of social grace. I should have said, "I can't talk to you now." The way I had said it, it sounded like I didn't want to talk to him ever again. Great. I noticed Kyle's Porsche wasn't in the garage when I went to get in my car. Maybe he spent the night at a friend's house. Or got home late and left early this morning. I would call him later.

I drove to where Ruby's house used to be. The streets of Nellie Gail Ranch were anything but deserted today. Lots of cars. The traffic worsened close to Ruby's place. The lookers were out en masse. It got so bad that I ended up parking my car on the side of the road and walking the last block. I saw workers busy installing a link fence around what once was Ruby's French chateau. The roof of the house had caved in. So had most walls. Only the brick chimney stood tall and straight, like a sentinel guarding the place. Part of the garage was left untouched, and you could see the charred remains of the Jeep. Mrs. Snoopy had described it accurately. If only that Jeep jammed against the garage door could talk. Yellow police tape warning people to stay away fluttered above the ashes in the morning breeze, along with the acrid smell of smoke lingering in the neighborhood.

I wanted to talk to somebody, ask questions. The uniformed people looked like fresh arrivals, and the rest of the crowd hoped to catch the show. I knocked at Mrs. Snoopy's door. Seemed like an eternity went by before she opened a few inches, recognized me and stepped out, closing the door behind her. She wasn't going to invite me in?

"Hi." She looked me over from behind her glasses. She wore a fussy dress, her hair was teased and sprayed and she had on full makeup. It was morning and she looked ready for a night at the opera.

"What happened?"

"Somebody burned the house down." Her response was matter-of-fact.

"Arson?"

I noticed the uneasiness. She avoided my eyes and readjusted her glasses. "I'm not supposed to discuss it. I already spoke to the police."

"The police told you not to discuss this?"

More hesitation. "Look, the lieutenant is on his way to see you and talk to your son. Ask him."

"My son? What does this have to do with my son?"

"Lieutenant Devin wants to talk to your son, the movie star."

She said "movie star" with such disdain I felt blood rushing to my face. Her expression changed and a slight smile appeared, but her eyes focused somewhere past me. I turned and it all became clear. A van with the Fox News logo parked around the corner. They'd come to interview her. I realized she said Devin, Lieutenant Devin. My Larry was on his way to my house—not to pursue a relationship with me, but to question Kyle about his involvement with Ruby's house burning down? I turned around and started to jog to my car. Why didn't he tell me he wanted to talk to me? Because I didn't let him. And she said he wanted to talk to Kyle. Larry had never met Kyle. This added puzzlement to my confusion.

I tried to process all the information, but my anger grew, and by the time my car crossed the gate to my townhouse I was in a pretty lousy mood. I entered the common garage expecting to find Larry's Mercedes taking up space. Instead, what I saw convinced me once again that life is never about what we anticipate, but rather about what we ignore. Right there, next to my reserved space, sat Ruby's Ferrari Testarossa.

NINE

My heels hit the path from the garage to my front door in unison with my heartbeat. Ruby, finally. Where could she be waiting for me? At the neighbors? She didn't have the keys to my place, she returned them. Could she have found a way to get into the house?

Strange.

I wanted to tell her about Larry, but first we needed to talk about Tom and the loss of her home, such terrible things. She needed a place to stay, of course. We would sit in the quietness of the living room, hug each other and exchange stories over a glass of Chardonnay. Everything would be okay. I opened the door wide and called out, "Ruby!"

I heard someone moving around upstairs, running down the steps, then Kyle appeared, smiling. "Hi, Mom, is Ruby here?"

"Kyle, you're here? I didn't see your car."

He looked at me, he seemed half amused, half apologetic. "About the car..."

I could hardly contain my newly found eagerness. I wanted to talk to Ruby. Kyle could tell me where he parked later.

"You did see my car in the garage." He dangled keys in front of my face. "A shiny Ferrari?"

"You bought the same car as the Russells?"

"No, I bought the Russells' car." He stared at me with those puppy eyes, waiting for a treat after a well-performed trick.

I felt sick. I sat and put my handbag on the floor, not sure what to do next. I must have looked awful, because Kyle came over and kneeled next to me. "Mom, are you okay?

What happened? You look like you've seen a ghost."

"A ghost of common sense. How, why? Tom's car? Did you buy it before or after Ruby shot him?" Did I say that? Ruby shot him? What was wrong with me?

"Ruby shot who? Mom, maybe you should lie down. You don't look too good." He helped me up from the chair and walked me over to the sofa. I let him lead me without arguing while my head reeled over this latest development.

"Kyle, you do know about Tom, don't you?"

He stared at me. I sensed his hesitation. He would choose his answer carefully, hoping not to say the wrong thing. He might be in his twenties, but he was still like a child reacting to his mother being upset with him. He didn't want to do or say the wrong thing.

"Tom is dead and the Russells' house burned to the ground last night." What I lacked in bedside manner I made up for with straight truth. I watched Kyle's face change expression and color faster than a chameleon sitting on a rainbow. He collapsed next to me on the sofa. I could hear the furious beating of his heart. I watched his Adam's apple bob when he swallowed.

"By the look on your face, I'm gathering the answer is no. You know nothing about anything." I thanked God for my self-control.

Kyle kept staring at his shoes.

"Kyle, Tom died a couple of days before I came back from Italy. I don't have many details. I'm guessing you didn't hear about it if you were in Palm Springs. It must have made only the local news. It was ruled an accidental death. Ruby reached for the gun Tom had been cleaning. The thing went off and hit Tom in the back of the skull. He died instantly. Here is my problem: I can't find Ruby. Do you know where she might be? When did you get the car? Kyle, where is your car?" Images of the Porsche parked in the garage the night before crossed my mind. I needed to let him talk. He rose and walked around the room. He looked like he was trying to work out the timeline for himself before telling me anything. I waited.

"We traded," he said.

"You traded what?"

"We traded cars, my Porsche for her Ferrari."

I shook my head. This was a car, not a toy. I couldn't believe he "traded" his car for hers so casually. I closed my eyes, found my composure and spoke with a strained voice. "Kyle, this is serious. You need to sit and tell me the whole story. Start from the beginning. I want dates and places. This is important." The last sentence came out a little louder than intended. He took a deep breath and launched into his story.

"Ruby came to Palm Springs. She showed up at the hotel, late, a few nights ago." He paused to count on his fingers. "Three nights ago. You know Ruby, all bubbly and excited, said she had to make a delivery for Tom out of state, Arizona, I think. She was on her way back and knew we were filming in Palm Springs, so she decided to stop and say hi."

"And?"

He paced, still avoiding my eyes. Not a good sign.

"Kyle," I shouted, and fought to control my voice. I could almost hear his brain processing what I had told him about the shooting, and wondering why Ruby hadn't mentioned it to him.

"That's why."

"Why what?"

"All the mystery, the games..." He looked straight into my eyes. "Ruby acted strangely the entire time she was there to see me. It felt uncomfortable. She cracked jokes and made her usual snarky comments, but she sounded different. Like her heart wasn't in it. She told me that the Ferrari had been broken into, things taken, and that Tom was mad. He wanted to get rid of the car. Pronto. She knew how much I liked the Testarossa and the fact that I was in Palm Springs was a good omen. Those were her exact words." Kyle cradled his head in his hands. "We had drinks in the hotel bar—she said she wanted a martini something bad—and then she got really sleepy. I had a suite, so I took her up to my room and let her crash on my bed. I ended up sleeping on the couch in the sitting area watching a movie. In fact, I slept terribly that night. My back was all kinked up from the couch, and I had a terrible headache. I arrived late to work since my alarm wasn't set." He got up and paced the room, avoided looking at me. "Ruby had left when I got up. There was an envelope on my night table, with the keys to the Ferrari and a note saying she had to go, she had taken the Porsche and we could work out the legalities later. I was going to call the Russells when you got home."

"The Russells' phone hasn't worked in days, and last night the house burned to the ground. Did you try her cell?"

His face turned white. He sat on the couch again, pulled something from his pants pocket and placed it on the coffee table. "Ruby's cell phone." He pointed to the small object he had laid next to the crystal bowl. "She left it in Palm Springs, in my hotel room."

A long pause. I waited.

"Did you say the house burned? How? Mom, you think it was an accident?"

We looked at each other, our eyes mirroring the same thoughts. How did the house burn? And where was Ruby with the Porsche?

"Kyle, I have a bad feeling about this whole situation. We need to tell the authorities. Did you check to see if Ruby left something else in the car?"

He shook his head. "I was so excited, wanted to show you the Ferrari. She never mentioned Tom being dead or her being the one who killed him. You think she's using?" He looked at me, searching my eyes for answers.

"You mean drugs? I doubt it. I haven't seen her in over a month, but I doubt it. Let's go take a look at the car, and we'll call the authorities. We can make a phone report of the car swap. And let's put her cell back in the glove compartment of the Ferrari. It's not our phone." We headed toward the door and I noticed Flash under the couch, watching us with a look of annoyance.

The underground common garage was always dark. Today wasn't any different. The white Ferrari created a bright spot. Kyle unlocked the driver's side and examined the glove compartment. I couldn't get myself to touch the damn thing.

"Anything?"

He wasn't listening. His eyes focused somewhere behind me, his whole expression morphing. I could swear even the color of his pupils grew darker.

I turned around.

Audrey, the next-door neighbor, breezed toward us. Where did she come from? It didn't seem to matter to Kyle. In his hurry to get out of the car I heard him hit his head on the metal doorframe. He didn't let out a sound. His face had the idiotic grin of a prime candidate for a broken heart.

She wore a dress made of a gauzy fabric, not short or fitted. The dress moved with her, fluttered around her lithe body, quivered with her every step. She carried some plastic grocery bags, her little brother tagging behind her, licking a lollipop.

"Hi!" My son offered her his hand. "Kyle York."

"Audrey Bernard." She smiled, bending a little forward to show that her arms were full of groceries.

He smiled back, and I felt invisible. I wasn't invisible to David. The kid flashed me a big grin. The contrast of his lips, bright red from the lollipop, against the pallor of his complexion somehow looked ghoulish. He noticed the Ferrari.

"Awesome!"

"You like it?" Kyle clicked something on the keys he held in his hand. The trunk opened, spooking David. The three of them laughed like old friends.

David craned his neck. "What's this?"

I looked. The plush carpeting covering the storage compartment of the trunk was ripped off on both sides.

I gawked at the sight. "What happened?"

"Thieves," Kyle concluded. "Tom's stereo equipment was stolen. That's why I got such a hot deal."

"Can I help you carry something?" Kyle glanced at Audrey.

She zapped him another smile and handed him one of the grocery bags. With David trotting behind them they walked toward Audrey's place, leaving me alone by the nefarious Ferrari. I assumed Kyle locked the car with his remote, as I walked back to my home alone and more confused than before.

Maybe Larry could—forget Larry. Wait a minute, Mrs. Snoopy told me that Devin was headed to my house. That was a long time ago, and by my personal clock it was an eternity. Did he change his mind?

Flash jumped on my lap, and I turned on the local news channel. They mentioned the house fire, and the fact that luckily there weren't any victims. No mention of foul play and no mention of Ruby missing either. Something wasn't right. How come no one seemed to be looking for Ruby? Larry never asked me if I knew where she was. Was she only hiding from me? Why? Hiding in plain sight? She was in Palm Springs three days ago and the Porsche was in my garage the night before. If Kyle hadn't been driving it, Ruby must have been here. SO, where was she now? She couldn't hide in the ashes of her house. Kyle asked me about the possibility of Ruby using drugs. I said no without hesitation. What made me such an expert? Ruby had these peculiar...episodes, had had them for four years—ever since Nick's death. Forgetting a whole day of her life. Buying things and then claiming someone else did it.

Six months before my recent trip to Florence, Ruby popped in, and I had to listen to her banking snafu.

"Lella, I'm losing it." She shouted the last words, and

her eyes had a feverish glow.

"What happened?" I rolled my eyes, unruffled by her sense of melodrama.

"I bounced a check, damn it." She clutched her glass of Chardonnay like a life preserver, her knuckles turning white.

"So? Is that all?" I laughed. "What's the big deal? Maybe Tom wrote a check and forgot to tell you."

"This is my personal account." She lowered her eyelids. "God's punishing me."

"Let's leave God out of the banking business."

"I wrote the check to my hairdresser. I got a notice this morning saying my account was overdrawn and I'd have to pay a penalty. I thought it was a mistake. I mean, such a small amount. I called the bank." The glass was still in her hands. "No mistake—at least, not from their end. The manager told me two more checks I'd recently written weren't going to be covered. I jumped in the car and drove down there." She drank the rest of the wine and handed me the empty glass.

Without a word, I went to refill it. Why would Ruby have her own account? I doubted she had any personal income. We'd been friends for years and she never mentioned a thing about this oh-so-personal account. Where did she get the money? Could it be severance pay from the Register? When I came back, Ruby was staring at a photo of Nick and me I kept on the Italian credenza. I gave her the glass, and she turned away from the picture, flushing. Perspiration had formed on her upper lip, and her skin glistened. Her hands trembled and the wine in the glass swashed around in slow motion, a lazy wave fading before reaching the shore.

"The teller showed me a large withdrawal. 'How did that happen?' I asked. She was nice about it. 'Ruby,' she said, 'you withdrew the money two days ago. Don't you remember? I had to okay it because you came in without your checkbook again. You were wearing a red dress.' I went home, saw my red dress in the dry cleaning pile and here I am."

"What did you do with the money?"

She didn't answer.

"You're getting all worked up over nothing. Tom will put money into your account to cover your bills. As for the rest, you're still going to experience memory gaps, but you said before you're having fewer. It takes time and patience. The doctor explained it to you from the beginning."

"If it weren't for Tom"—she paused—"and you, I would have put an end to this a long time ago."

"Ruby, you're alive." I stopped short of adding that Nick wasn't so lucky. I knew she sensed it.

She nodded and left.

It wasn't like Ruby to have money and an account she never spoke of. A personal account; pocket change or big bucks? Maybe she needed it for a sense of security. Why? She had Tom for that.

They'd met about the time I started making potpourri sachets for the gift shop at the mission. Ruby was still wearing her neck collar back then. It made it hard for her to drive, especially in reverse. She'd just left her doctor's office and was backing out of her parking spot when she hit Tom's car, a white Ferrari Testarossa. Stuff dreams are made of.

I sighed, enough dreaming for today. I didn't know how long I had been sitting and reminiscing. The room flaunted an early shade of dusk, and my body and spirit felt fully drained, refusing to move, almost in a daze. I still had no idea how the Porsche ended up in the parking garage the night before, only to be gone by morning.

The front door swung open, and Kyle pranced in. "Mom, why didn't you tell me about your neighbor? She's great."

I sensed that wasn't the original description he had in mind, but even in the dimness of the living room he must have noticed the fire shooting from my eyes.

"Kyle, dear God, is that all you can think about?" I knew as soon as I said it that it wasn't fair to lash out at Kyle because I was frustrated.

But instead of answering my question he launched into Audrey's bio without pausing to ask if I cared to listen.

"Do you know that Audrey used to live in Arizona? She was telling me about high school kids going down there from California during spring break. She may drive over to Palm Springs and watch us filming. David, her little brother, would come along, and then we'll all take a ride to Arizona. I've never been there." At some point he must have realized this was a one-way conversation, because he stopped talking for a minute and then shifted gears. "What's the matter, Mom? Are you still concerned about the Ferrari? Don't worry. I'll get everything straightened out, I promise. In the meantime, are you hungry? Want to go grab something to eat down at the marina? Maybe Audrey will join us. Hey, stop with the eyes already. Don't look so upset."

The phone rang.

"I'll get it." He rushed over to the house phone. "York residence. Carolyn, it's me. What do you mean where in the hell am I? At my mother's house. You called here. Oh, I forgot to charge it. That's why it goes to voice mail. Sorry. Okay, don't get so ticked off. No, I didn't forget. I was on my way out the door. Yes, I'll be there soon." He hung up. "Shit, I'd forgotten all about meeting Carolyn. I've got to get out of here." He ran upstairs.

Carolyn, his agent. He'd probably forgotten some social event. In their world, social commitments were as important as business meetings. In fact, there wasn't one without the other. Kyle came back, his overnighter under his arm, clothes spilling out.

"Sorry about the mess I left, Mom. I'll make it up to you." He walked by the kitchen and grabbed a banana. "Can you tell Audrey—never mind. I'll call her. Got to run. Ciao." He slammed the door shut.

I ran after him and caught him by the car. "Kyle, we need to resolve the car situation. It's important. Where are you heading?"

"LA. I'll be back tomorrow. I'll stop by on my way back. Smile, Mom. It's going to be okay." He smiled, and I shook my head, smiling back. I watched the white Ferrari Testarossa drive up the road to the gate and decided to check my mail before going back into the house for the evening. The beauty of the sun setting over the Pacific soothed me a little. I realized I hadn't thought about Nick until just then. I wasn't sure if that was good or bad. The complex looked deserted. Not surprising, since it was dinner time. Dinner for one would be what came next in my empty house. Stop feeling sorry for yourself, Lella. The lights came on, intensifying the hues of the setting sun against the white walls of the villas.

I rounded the corner and stopped. There stood the man I had been thinking about more than I should have, Larry Devin.

TEN

His hand rested on my knee, the same spot as the night of the kiss. "Rested" didn't describe the feelings that simple contact stirred up. We'd been driving in silence for maybe half an hour, and my head swirled with dozens of questions, questions I couldn't find the nerve to put into words. I kept the conversation in neutral, ignoring the furious thumping of my heart.

"Where are we going?"

"Orange."

"Orange? We're in Orange County right now, aren't we?"

"The town of Orange. Are you hungry?"

"Famished. I skipped lunch. I was too busy with Kyle, my son—"

"How about we forget about family and friends for tonight? The day is almost over. Let's celebrate the evening, and I can promise you all the issues, the problems we left behind tonight, will be there in the morning. Deal?"

"Deal." Did he say in the morning? He assumed I would spend the night with him? I couldn't possibly do that. I wasn't prepared for an overnight stay. It all happened so quickly that in the excitement of the moment I forgot to take my cell phone. Did I feed Flash before rushing out the door? If Larry sensed my hesitation, he didn't acknowledge it. His hand went from my knee to my cheek. He had this way of stroking my face with the back of his fingers, such intense tenderness. I wished I could stop the passing seconds, encapsulate the moment, so I could revisit that bewitching feeling in times of loneliness. Ah, those magic fingers must have the power to stop intelligent thoughts from becoming spoken words and also made the lack of cell phone or overnight necessities seem okay, because I didn't object about a thing.

We left the freeway and traveled a street I didn't recognize. Few cars passed us in either direction. I couldn't see any shape of buildings, only lights fleeing by. With the speed of the Mercedes, lamp posts looked like fireflies on a caffeine rush. The road narrowed to a single lane, and we climbed a hill. Gravel skittered under the tires. Both sides of the road had tall trees, so tall and so perfectly spaced they formed a natural canopy.

What was a good Italian Catholic woman doing here with this man of mystery, anyway? The real question pounding my mind was: What was this fascinating man of mystery doing with this silly, love-struck widow?

The sight of a gate interrupted my mental tug of words. Not a fancy or elaborate gate like the one at my complex, but a simple, sturdy-looking metal barrier. Larry reached overhead, hitting a button, and the gate opened slowly, no grinding or squeaking. It whirred quietly, and we drove through the yawning gap. He must have heard my involuntary gulping.

"I live here."

I realized we were high on a hill, and I could see thousands of lights twinkling below. I searched frantically for something to say, something to ask, but all I came up with was, "Uh, huh."

"And no, I didn't buy the house with the cash from the lottery." I sensed a smile in his voice. He'd answered what was going to be my next question. He reached for something above his head again, and the hill in front of us became alive with lights, the gurgling of a fountain and a garage door opening to let the Mercedes in.

I followed him up two steps and then through a door that led to a laundry room the size of my kitchen, but with a lot more cabinetry. From there we went into a large room with tall windows and taller walls.

It must be what real estate agents call "a great room," but it was more than great. It was grand. My prediction of a seduction chamber died at the sight of the contemporary chairs and couch that weren't made of black leather, the common denominator of bachelor pads. I saw white linen with huge, overstuffed pillows. I moved slowly, feeling awkward and out of place.

Not knowing what to do with myself, I followed Larry like a puppy exploring new surroundings. We turned a corner and I noticed a baby grand piano in the farthest side of the great room. Larry played the piano? We reached the kitchen, also white and wonderful, like the ones in the home and garden magazines Ruby subscribed to. Wait until Ruby heard about my escapade.

Larry removed his suede bomber jacket and dropped it casually on one of the tall kitchen stools lined up against the huge kitchen island. He opened the door of the side-by-side freezer. The light reflected on his shirt, forming a whimsical aura around his silhouette.

"Lella, you can choose what you like to eat."

"You're going to cook?" My voice grated into my ears in the expanse of the room.

"No, it's already cooked and labeled. Pick what you want, it goes in the oven and we can eat in about thirty minutes."

I didn't move.

"Lella, I have a couple who comes once a week. Peter cleans the house, Jim does the cooking and the laundry. They're good people. I've known them for over ten years. The food isn't poisoned." The smile lingered on his lips, but his eyes studied me. I stepped forward and he moved from the freezer. "You pick the meal you want and I'll get the wine. You okay?"

I nodded and read the labels. Quite an impressive menu. All neatly pre-packaged so that whomever Larry brought home could admire the set-up. Why was I so angry? I was angry because I stepped into his car anticipating some kind of sexual overture. Instead he offered a TV dinner and a glass of wine. I pulled out a baking dish labeled PORK CHOPS AND POTATOES. It seemed like a safe choice.

"Got it." I turned, but the kitchen was empty. That was when I noticed the photograph on the refrigerator door. It was a picture of Larry sitting next to a gorgeous girl, half my age and, at first glance, a natural blonde.

I stood, holding the frozen dish in my hands, asking myself once again what the hell I was doing there.

"That's Olivia, my daughter." I hadn't heard him approach.

"I didn't know you had a daughter."

"Yes, there's a lot you don't know about me. We have all the time you want. Ask away."

"Olivia," I repeated. "She lives with you?"

"Sometimes. Right now she's backpacking through Europe with a friend." He pointed to the baby grand. "That's hers."

"You're divorced?"

"No."

"Married?" I wanted to die the minute I asked—before hearing the assumed answer.

"No. It happened in college. We both knew we made a mistake, but we decided to keep the baby. We have a friendly relationship and joint custody. Olivia's mother lives in Florida with her husband of fifteen years. How about I take that dish before your fingers freeze?"

I handed him the food and walked away. I didn't want to be here, in his house. I wanted to go home. I wanted the home-turf advantage. Home-turf advantage for what? I walked to the massive window, where I could see the lawn and the fountain we passed driving up to the house. Outside that circle of light I saw only darkness.

"I have quite a view by daylight." He stood behind me and again. I hadn't heard him approach. Was he barefooted? I turned to glance at his feet, and my head hit the stem glass in his hand. He reacted quickly, so the wine spilled on the wooden floor instead of his shirt.

"I'm so sorry."

"You should be. It's your glass. Mine is over there." He smiled at me.

"Where can I get a rag to clean up?" I found it difficult to talk, embarrassment flooding my brain.

"Lella, a few drops of wine isn't going to ruin the floor. Forget about it. Let's sit down, relax and enjoy our drinks until the food is ready." He took my hand and walked me over to the linen couch. I envisioned myself spilling wine on the white cover.

"The slipcover is machine washable."

He had all the answers, while I felt totally out of place without knowing why.

"I'm going home." I didn't have the pluck to look at him. "Where did I put my purse?"

I moved slightly and he stood. "Lella." He put his hand on my shoulder.

"Don't touch me." I pushed him with both fists. He fell back on the couch and I fell with him, my face inches from his. We looked at each other, my furor to his coolness, my transparency to his secrecy, my insecurity to his boldness. Our mouths locked and none of it mattered. Like in the car, tasting his lips, I felt more urgency.

His body slid from the couch to the floor, taking me with him. His erection pressing against my belly aroused my lust to the point of physical pain. I put my hands on his shoulders and pushed myself away from him. I savored the wetness of our kiss, inhaled the scent of his aftershave and the scent of his skin.

His hands traveled the length of my body, reached my elbows and gently nudged me away. We looked at each other without smiling, the want in his eyes as heady as the need I felt. He moved so that we lay side by side, facing each other. I didn't want any space between us. I wanted my body against his. I kicked off my shoes without changing position and locked my legs around his, drawing him even closer. The fabric from his slacks felt warm and soft and I found myself stroking the cloth, back and forth, with my toes.

He cupped my face in his hands, tilted my head back and brushed my throat with his lips. Eyes closed, I felt his fingers move under my dress, forcing it off my shoulders. When he unhooked the front clasp my bra slid off my hard nipples. It occurred to me in that instant that I used to fantasize and hope, without much conviction, about finding passion and desire again, at least once, before getting too old to care. Here I was, drowning in passion and desire, the need for sex so strong my whole body quivered in anticipation.

I pulled his shirt from the waist of his pants without undoing his belt and began to unbutton it. I was a woman on a mission, and I soon had him barechested. I put my hands on his belt buckle, hesitated an instant and then moved to the zipper. His hands beat me to it. I heard his shoes hit the floor and when I opened my eyes he was totally naked next to me.

I wiggled out of my dress and dropped myself on top of him. My nipples brushed his chest, and he shivered. We looked at each other, our eyes filled with a new haste, our bodies throbbing in anticipation. I arched my back and guided his hands to my hips. He gently pulled down my lace panties. His hardness pressed against my flesh. I reached my first climax before he fully entered me. When I bit his neck to muffle my scream, somewhere in the white kitchen the oven bell chimed.

ELEVEN

I woke and for a moment didn't recognize anything, including the room. Then I remembered I was in Larry's bed. In the dim light of the early morning I found myself alone. No sign of Larry. I was not a morning person, but I felt wide awake. Too nervous to try to go back to sleep, I listened to the silence of this house, a house I didn't know any more than I knew its master.

With my eyes closed, I relived the moments of the night. I couldn't remember how we went from the main room to this bed, but I clearly remembered the unending hunger of our bodies and the sense of content fulfillment I felt before surrendering to sleep. The absence of sounds in the house puzzled me. So Larry had no pets—oh, no. Flash. I forgot about my cat. Did I fill her dish with dry food before I left for the evening? I had to get home. Larry would have to drive me.

I craned my neck in hope to see if he was in the bathroom. Where could he be? His scent lingered on me like a second skin, yet I couldn't get myself to call his name. After hours of lustful sex, conflicting feelings crowded my mind, and I had more unanswered questions now than before. And for the icing on the cake, this was the dreaded morning after.

Enough with the bashful modesty. I stepped out of bed and headed straight for the shower. I couldn't tell if Larry had used it before me. It looked staged for a glossy cover of House Beautiful. And this obsession with white—white towels, white marble floors. Between the double sinks sat a silver tray with toothbrush, comb and miniature bottles of toiletries. I kept a similar stash in my guest room. We spent the night in his guest room?

Wrapped in one of the comfy white bath sheets, I went back into the bedroom and saw that my clothes, including my lingerie, were folded and stacked neatly on a small bench by a large, round window that dominated the room. The view was breathtaking, and I heard birds singing in the trees dotting the property. What a neat freak Larry appeared to be, with all the spotless white and the orderly folded clothing. Living with such perfection day in and day out would drive me batty.

I dressed in last night's clothes; when I pulled up the zipper to my dress, the smell of freshly brewed coffee hit me. I didn't want to look in the mirror. I didn't like my looks in the morning, and without my faithful lotions and potions I felt exposed.

Barefoot, I followed the aroma of coffee and soon heard Larry's voice coming from the kitchen. I tiptoed in, not sure what kind of welcome awaited me. He was fully dressed, shaved and apparently conducting business. All this before 8:00 a.m.

He stood on the inside of the kitchen island opposite the barstools, talking on the phone, a pad and pen in front of him. When he noticed me standing there, he winked and motioned me to sit. I perched on a kitchen stool and waited for a smile, a nod, something more than a wink to let me know our hours of passion meant more than an elaborate one-night stand.

Larry appeared to be focused on whoever was on the other end of the phone. "Okay then, we'll see you soon. Thanks." He put the phone down and turned to look at me, a wry smile on his face. "Lella, we need to talk."

Those few words were all I needed for my insecurities to sneak back into the kitchen and reclaim my brain. I felt ugly, old and more than a little pathetic in yesterday's clothes.

"Oh." I sighed.

"You don't think I'm a detective, huh? Because of my

lifestyle? What? You can't solve crimes unless you live in a crime-ridden neighborhood?"

Blood rushed to my face. I gulped air and averted my eyes from his.

"I'm not going to bother asking you where you got your information. I was a homicide detective for nearly twenty years. I still am, but on extended leave of absence, without pay, I may add, by choice. The day I came to your house was my last day at work. I'll give you that I have nothing to do with the Russells' case. Then again, there really isn't a case." He pushed an empty cup in my direction, poured coffee and placed cream and sugar next to it. "Tom's death was an accident, and the books were closed, but apparently a neighbor kept calling and fussing about the department not doing a thorough investigation. I was going to be in Dana Point the next day, so I told my sergeant I would talk to you—the one person we didn't interview, sort of a goodwill gesture to keep the Russells' neighbor happy."

"Mrs. Snoopy." I found my voice.

"Mrs. who?"

"The woman living across from the Russells. She came over to talk to me when I went looking for Ruby." Was I imagining things? His whole demeanor shifted when I mentioned Ruby. "You said it wasn't your case, yet you were back there after the fire. Talking to Mrs. Snoopy again."

"Are you conducting your own investigation?" His voice sounded detached, but I could tell he was ticked off at me. Without saying another word he gathered his pen and pad, then stopped and looked at me, his eyes dark slivers of complexity.

"Let's have some coffee and toast. That's all we have time for. We need to get to Santa Ana before 9:00 a.m., and traffic is heavy this time of day."

"I need to get home. I'm not sure if I left enough food for my cat."

He must have thought I was making up an excuse to

leave, as I'd done last night. He came to my side and drew me into his arms. Larry put his fingers under my chin to lift my face and kissed me on the mouth. A light kiss, closed lips, yet he lingered and in a fleeting moment I thought that if he let go of the kiss it would mean letting go of us.

"Lella"—I was still a happy prisoner of his embrace—"we need to talk about Kyle."

I freed myself from his arms so I could look at him. "You know my son? I had no idea."

"I don't know him personally. But Kyle got himself in trouble." He kept his face above mine, his mouth in my hair.

"What kind of trouble?" I couldn't tell how serious this was.

Larry disentangled himself and walked away. He avoided looking at me.

"Aren't you going to answer? What kind of trouble has Kyle gotten into?" I was madly curious, and very concerned. But he wasn't talking. How dare he? We didn't say anything else. We drank our coffee in silence, sort of waiting each other out. When he headed out the door I followed.

I wondered if Kyle had been caught speeding as usual and got pulled over in Tom and Ruby's car without the necessary paperwork. A strong possibility. We walked the same wide corridor we'd come through the evening before. He entered a door next to the bedroom we slept in. I glimpsed a room on the opposite side of the hall. It looked like an office, with a large desk facing the windows. The view was spectacular, but that hadn't been what stopped me. A flat-screen computer monitor sat atop the desk. From the screen, in full color, Ruby smiled at me. No sound, just the image. I stood on the threshold, too stunned to move.

"It's my office." Larry's voice came from behind me. As usual, I didn't hear him approach.

"That's Ruby." I found myself whispering, not sure why.

"Yes, I know. I keep my computer on my department website. The site isn't available to the public. Old habit. This morning Ruby Russell showed up as 'missing.'"

"It's about time."

"Why do you say that?"

"I've been trying to find her since I returned from Italy. I was beginning to wonder why I'm the only one who doesn't know where she is."

"Are you saying you haven't seen her since your trip? Aren't you two best friends?" Something in his voice alerted me that he knew a lot more about my so-called best friend than he was telling me. He put his hand on my arm. I fought the urge to brush it off, instead I let him guide me back to the kitchen.

"Yes, that's precisely what I'm saying. What happened to make the police decide she's missing?"

"Concern, I suppose. After the house fire they may have tried to find her to let her know. I don't have those details."

"She was in Palm Springs three days ago. She went to visit Kyle, and he let her talk him into exchanging cars without transferring the paperwork."

Larry grabbed my arm hard. He spun me to face him. "Lella, we need to get going right now. Kyle is due in court this morning. You've got to tell Bonnie what you just told me before the arraignment."

"Who's Bonnie and what's this about an arraignment? Was Kyle arrested because of the Ferrari? "

"We'll talk in the car. It's very important we leave now."

"Important to whom? I want some explanation. Stop with the half-truths. Who are you protecting?"

"Lella, please. Time is of the essence. For Kyle. We must get going. You can get mad at me, it's okay, but we need to talk to Bonnie before court."

I picked up my purse and found my high-heel sandals under the couch in the main room. My stomach gurgled; maybe it was hunger mixed with anger and fear. I wished I'd eaten the toast. Larry came from the back room ready to go.

We got into the Mercedes and dashed through the gate,

leaving the house on the hill at a dizzying speed. Larry didn't say a thing until we exited the one lane road and entered the Costa Mesa Freeway.

"Lella, the information regarding Kyle and the car could make a big difference with how the arraignment goes for him."

"Stop treating me like I'm some simpering child. What's going on?"

"Arraignment is when a person accused of something goes in front of a judge and there's one lawyer representing the state and one representing the accused. They both tell their side, and the judge decides if there is enough evidence to keep the person in jail. The judge also decides if bail should be granted or if the case should be dismissed altogether. Bonnie Fisher is the lawyer representing your son. She's the best in the business. Keep your fingers crossed."

"Evidence for what? What did Kyle do? How do you know all this?" My voice had an edge, the edge of panic. I was being punished for spending the night with Larry.

"Lella, Kyle was driving Ruby's Ferrari when he got pulled over. There was an alert out for the car. His arrest was posted on my computer like everything else that comes through the department."

"And you didn't tell me?"

"I'm telling you now. Tell me the details about the car swap."

"Why can't this Bonnie get the case dismissed? It's his car now. Ruby's driving his Porsche." Now the panic in my voice resounded loud and clear.

"Since we can't find Ruby, she can't corroborate his story. All we can hope is a judge will see this is a simple misunderstanding and release Kyle on bail until we sort through it. Lella, I'm on your side. Talk to me."

I repeated the sequence of events just as Kyle had told me. I even explained that I felt we needed to get a pink slip for the car, so that there would be no doubts. Not that I approved of the exchange, but it was what Ruby and Kyle had worked out.

By now I recognized some of the street signs and knew we were approaching Santa Ana. We didn't speak for a long time, and I was getting more and more fearful. Larry kept his hand on my knee. I was sure it was meant to be a comforting gesture, but it wasn't working.

What had Kyle gotten himself into? By now he must have explained to the police about exchanging cars with Ruby. With all the computers, the cell phones and cameras on every street corner, the police should have found ways of verifying his story. That's what they do on those investigative shows on television. Something didn't feel right. Either Larry didn't know the whole story, or he wasn't telling me everything. Kyle must have been pulled over right after he left my house. What if he tried to call me? Had it not been for Larry, I would have been there to answer the phone. Dio mio. What else was Larry hiding from me? Too many coincidences. Did he set me up? That didn't make sense either. My heart thumped erratically against my throat. How was it possible? Twenty-four hours ago I was bitching about my ordinary life. I deserved the punishment but Kyle had done nothing, nothing worth jail time.

The residential street we drove on looked peaceful, but the older homes were now offices, and the majority housed lawyers. Larry slowed down in front of a two-story home on the corner, pulled into the driveway and circled to the back of the house. Still silent, he came around, opened the passenger door then escorted me through the back door of the light green house.

We walked on plank floors, shiny and sturdy, into a room that may once have been a parlor but now appeared to be a sunny office.

"There you are. I was getting nervous. This must be Mrs. York, Kyle's mom?" The woman giving the welcome speech didn't look like a lawyer to me; she wasn't at all what I had expected. A little taller than me, pudgy, but in an endearing sort of way. I couldn't tell why, but I liked her. Gray and blond hair fought for dominance, the gray apparently winning. No tailored suit. Instead, loose brown slacks, flat shoes and a soft beige sweater. Comfort clothes.

What were we waiting for?

"Bonnie, Lella has an interesting story to tell you about Kyle and the Ferrari. It may change the whole picture, for the better."

I heard tension in Larry's voice and it surprised me. Why would he be tense? This was about my son, not his. And I felt something else too: a connection between Larry and Bonnie, some kind of unspoken sense of personal awareness, a subtle familiarity that opposite sexes usually acquire while sharing the same sheets. Were they lovers? Past or present? I couldn't tell.

Bonnie glanced at my little black dress. "We need to get you something else to wear for court." I felt heat rush to my face and I lowered my eyes. Yesterday's clothes.

She left the office and came back in less than a minute. She handed me a simple gray sweater. "This will tone you down a bit. It belongs to my secretary She is petite, like you. It should fit."

I had to roll up the sleeves once I put the sweater on, but I welcomed the more appropriate look and was thankful for it. Larry watched the whole scene without interfering. Bonnie turned to him.

"Larry, you should leave. It's better if we go without you. I'm taking Mrs. York with me. I'll call you when it's over."

He walked over and kissed me. He kissed me on the lips, right there in front of Bonnie, and the gesture shocked me. I stood, feeling awkward. A mannequin in the wrong window.

He must have mistaken my unease because he

reassured me, "You'll be fine, Lella. Bonnie will take care of you and Kyle. Don't be scared, okay?"

In that instant I told myself that perhaps Larry did care a little about me, and somehow the pain eating away at my heart became a bit more bearable.

TWELVE

Twenty-five minutes. That was how long I'd been sitting in the busy courtroom. I begged Bonnie to let me see Kyle, but she insisted it wasn't possible. She convinced me to sit and wait, for Kyle's own good.

All types of people came and went: lawyers, their clients, anxious family members trying to lend support. Bonnie warned me I might have to wait. She told me where to sit, then disappeared somewhere to talk to Kyle. I was glad I wore that borrowed sweater. I felt too easily noticed in my fitted black dress. More time went by. Where was my son? The tension brought on by the wait had me feeling sick. I tried to control my nervous fidgeting. I needed to see Kyle. Assure myself he was all right, at least physically. All the things I read in the papers about Orange County prisons flashed through my mind. Prisoners getting stabbed, punched, killed. Please, God, Kyle is a good kid. I'm the sinner.

To control my despair I shifted my attention to the surroundings. The female judge had a perfect bob and her nails sported a French manicure. Before rendering a verdict, she tented her hands and rested her chin on them. I became so fascinated by the process I hadn't noticed that Bonnie had come back and sat next to me.

"How are you holding up?"

I shook my head, swallowing my tears. "Did you see Kyle?"

"He's in show business." Bonnie sighed—she wasn't happy or even excited to have such a clean-cut client. No, her sigh and facial expression conveyed: Crap, why me? Another Hollywood idiot who got caught.

"Is this bad? That he's in the movies?" What difference

did it make? Kyle was an actor, booking a few commercials and even a semi-regular part on a soap opera. Would his on-screen persona alter the judge's feelings toward him? She probably didn't know anything about his background.

"The whole California judiciary system is still under scrutiny for the questionable outcomes of the Simpson, Blake and Jackson trials."

"Mio dio, Bonnie, my son is accused of stealing a car, not murder. I explained to you about the car swap." Bonnie gave me a look.

"What exactly did Larry tell you Kyle was accused of?"

I shrugged, trying not to look too defensive. "Larry didn't tell me anything. He just said this was all a misunderstanding."

Bonnie rolled her eyes. "A misunderstanding? That's rich. Add kidnapping to the car theft and we are getting closer."

I didn't understand her impatience. She had to know I wasn't used to appearing in court. Kidnapping? Nonsense.

"Who are they saying Kyle kidnapped? That's insane." None of my remarks seemed to ruffle her. Maybe she was getting her clients mixed up.

"Lella, now you need to pay attention. Kyle is up next. It's good that he sees a familiar face. He needs to know we are here for him. You won't be able to speak to him. Are you listening? This is extremely important. I don't want you to disrupt court proceedings; it would go against what we are trying to accomplish—"

"What are we trying to accomplish?" I felt so lost.

"To have Kyle released, of course. What do you think we're trying to do?" While talking, her eyes kept scanning the room, like a general inspecting the battlefield before combat.

"Damn! The jig is up. Lella, don't turn around to look."

"Look for what, for whom?" No food all day and with the adrenaline pumping at full speed, I felt loopy.

"TMZ is in the building." Bonnie drummed her fingers on her briefcase then noted my blank look. "TMZ reports all kind of news regarding show business. They are fast and accurate. I bet they're the first press here. I recognize one of their minions. Don't look. I don't want them to know who you are. Paparazzi." She mumbled, shaking her head, and surveyed the people around us again.

Bonnie said, "Okay, we're up next. Remember what I told you. Smile and that's it. Don't leave your seat." She took two steps toward one of the tables used by lawyers. At the same time, from a side door, men in uniform escorted Kyle in.

My reaction was to run and hug him and tell him everything would be all right, but I remembered Bonnie's warning. I sat, my eyes transfixed on the orange-clad child of mine shuffling toward Bonnie's table. At first I thought he had a limp. Then I realized his stilted walk was due to the shackles locked to his ankles. The pieces of my broken heart weighed on my chest, and I lost the fight against my tears.

Kyle noticed me right away. He nodded his head in a sign of recognition and attempted a smile, but he was too tense to do more than bare his teeth at me. I knew that, like me, he had no idea what this was all about. I was left swallowing my tears while staring at Bonnie and Kyle's backs. The lawyer for the prosecution was a tall man with very dark hair and an air of extreme confidence, though not necessarily genuine. He spoke in a loud voice, enunciating every word. Quite a contrast with Bonnie's soft voice and non-confrontational attitude.

I heard the word come out of the man's mouth: "Kidnapping."

No. It hit me so hard I could hardly make out what Bonnie replied. "No risk," she was saying.

I noticed Kyle's shoulders slump. My son never slouches. My son is proud of who he is and what he does. I stood, ready to shout. The judge gave me a curious glance. Bonnie turned around to glare at me, and I dropped back into to my seat. By the time I was able to breathe halfway normally, the judge's hands were tented and I knew my son wouldn't be driving home with me. No bail.

Bonnie whispered something to Kyle, patting him on the arm. He turned to look at me and made a small gesture with his hand, sort of a goodbye wave. The guards took an arm each and he started the shuffle back toward the same door he had come from.

I sat motionless. A frozen, useless old woman who couldn't even help her only child. I didn't want to move, only wanted to close my eyes. I wanted to feel the touch of a friendly hand, a friendly voice telling me everything would be fine. Instead I heard Bonnie's voice, angry and nearly shouting; she was arguing with the tall lawyer with the dark hair and loud voice. I cursed Bonnie for letting this happen to my son and I cursed Larry for lying to me about Bonnie being "the best in the business." But I mostly cursed at myself for bringing Ruby into Kyle's life.

"Let's go." Bonnie grabbed my arm and practically lifted me from the chair. "We're going out through a different exit. I don't want to fight the media."

I had a hard time keeping up with her and couldn't ask any questions. We were practically running through a narrow, windowless corridor. And then we were in the parking garage. Inside her car, she told me to stay down. I could tell cameras flashed as we exited the building and hit the road.

"You can sit up now." Her cell phone went off, startling me.

"Yeah. No. She's in the car with me. Crap, Larry, you could have told me the kid's in show biz. Yeah, freaking paparazzi. It doesn't matter. By now they've figured out she's the mother. Look, this is a lot worse than... They don't have much, but enough to deny bail, for now. I need to gather some information. I'm going to need you to make some calls. It's a gimmick. They want him there while they collect evidence, build their case against him. I'm on my way back to the office. No, don't come there. Better if we keep you out of the picture." Finally she hung up.

"I'm going home." Deep-seated anger replaced my sense of worthless.

"Not a good idea." Bonnie's voice was soft and pleasant again.

"I'm going home," I repeated, my eyes on the road. "I need to fix this."

She patted my leg, and I asked myself if she picked up the habit from Larry. "I'm not going to try to talk you out of it, Lella. I understand how you feel, but there may be reporters waiting for you at your house. You're not used to this kind of situation, and it can get ugly."

"No, you don't understand how I feel. Don't patronize me. What kind of law is this? My son didn't do a thing to Ruby. She's hiding. I don't know why, but I intend to find out. As for the media, I'll take my chances. I'll need a taxi."

Bonnie parked in the back parking lot of her office. Everything was the same as it was this morning with Larry. Everything but me. She convinced me to keep the sweater, saying I could return it later. Bonnie was kind enough to arrange for her assistant to drive me home. It would be a long ride, and I was thankful. Then she handed me a cell phone. "Here. I want you to have this. It's disposable. Only Larry and I have the number, so make sure you answer when it rings. We have work to do. Let's get that kid of yours out of jail."

"Bonnie." I looked straight into her eyes. "Aside from the nonsense of the kidnapping, exactly what is Kyle accused of doing to Ruby?"

"He got picked up last night for driving a stolen car. Ruby's Ferrari. The charges as of now are car theft and, yes, kidnapping. Being accused of kidnapping Ruby Russell is the excuse to keep him in jail until they'll come up with something else. Think about it, what happens after a person gets kidnapped?" She didn't wait for an answer.

I wept quietly in the car. It was awkward being driven home by a stranger and not being able to stop crying. I asked the young lady to let me off way before the gate. I figured if the media was waiting, they'd be looking for me to arrive by car. They would be either by the gate or outside the garage watching my door. I let myself in through a pedestrian side gate used mostly by landscapers and other service people, walked past the complex's pool and hopped over the low fence surrounding the neighbor's yard.

I entered my place from the back door and no one saw me. My drapes were drawn from the night before. Flash heard me and rushed over to welcome me. I rubbed her back and went straight upstairs to my closet. I found my winter coat, the one I had packed instead of wearing for the trip back from Florence. My hands shook so badly I had trouble getting into the pockets. Dio mio, found it. My fingers felt the paper. I pulled it out and unfolded it on the bed. The cell phone chimed in the depth of my handbag. I ignored it.

I ran my fingers over the chart, Ruby's chart, and I sobbed. There weren't enough tears in the universe to wash away my guilt. How could I spend the night with a man I hardly knew while this man's buddies dragged my son to prison? How?

My sense of reality faded in and out, caught in a twist of memories. Why, Ruby? Why? Was this misguided revenge? Against Kyle, or was she using my son to get to me? What was it that I didn't see? Maybe this had nothing to do with her brain injury. Perhaps she didn't change, just stopped pretending.

I thought about those months after Nick's death—the emptiness left in my heart.

I'd packed up the house, sold it, sent Nick's things to storage. Then I'd gone back to Italy, unable to bear being here alone. When I'd finally come back, I had no place of my own.

Then, too, Kyle had picked me up at LAX.

Kyle and I both avoided the subject of Nick and Ruby, keeping the conversation superficial and chatty. "You can stay at my place, Mom. I'll be in San Francisco the next few weeks." Kyle's career had taken off, and he worked on location most of the time. This time the location happened to be San Francisco, a one-hour flight from Los Angeles.

I'd done just that. After Kyle left for San Francisco, I spent the next week lying in bed, not even getting dressed. I mainly wore pajamas or sweatpants. I ate the food I found in his fridge. Didn't turn on the lights or the television. I felt inconsequential and sort of embraced the feeling. I supposed it was a natural reaction after being married for such a long time and doing everything as a couple.

Kyle's telephone rang constantly, and I listened to the messages that the callers, mostly female, left. The information ranged from sweet and simple to outrageous to vulgar.

Ruby called on the fourth day of my self-imposed solitude. I didn't pick up. Even when I heard Ruby say: "Kyle, this is Ruby. I heard Lella's back. How is she? Can I have her phone number? She must have changed the other one I had. Call me. Thanks."

Listening to her voice after all that time had brought a sense of fury into my consciousness. From the police report and from Kyle, I'd learned Nick was driving Ruby's car with Ruby in the passenger seat. It was unclear where they were going. Or what they were doing together. I chose the cowardly way out and never asked. What you don't know can't hurt, I told myself back then. I still did that sometimes.

I screamed at the answering machine, at the walls and at the unfairness of the whole wide world.

She called again the next day and the next...

I seemed to live only for her calls.

On the eighth day Ruby called in the morning. She sounded increasingly annoyed, as if trying to guess whether

Kyle was out of town or ignoring her messages.

I sat in the dark, hugging a pillow and feeling sorry for myself and, as I often did, wishing Ruby had died instead of Nick.

Twenty minutes later, the phone rang again. Ruby. She repeated word for word what she'd said in her very first message. Goose bumps bristled on my skin, and I felt the urge to open the window wide and let the sunshine in. I got dressed and went shopping. Anything to get away from Ruby's calls. I didn't buy a thing.

That night she phoned very late. Her annoyance was replaced with fear. "Kyle, something's happened to Lella. You've got to come down here immediately. I stopped by her house to say hello, and a strange woman opened the door. She wouldn't let me in. I'm worried about your mother. Should I call the police? No. I tell you what. I'll get myself back there, sit in my neighbors' car and watch the house until you get here."

Click.

Cold sweat covered my forehead and the back of my neck. She was crazy. I'd sold my house months ago. I became so distraught I couldn't think...I had to talk to somebody.

Anybody but Ruby. I put on the dress I wore on the flight home, grabbed my still unpacked luggage and left Kyle's apartment.

I checked into the Holiday Inn then called my son in San Francisco.

He didn't sound surprised.

He said he understood my anger and my blaming Ruby for the accident. If Nick hadn't been driving her car, if he hadn't been traveling with her in the first place, the accident might have never happened. He figured it was time to tell me what was wrong with Ruby.

She couldn't drive yet and was often confused. After she appeared to have an epileptic seizure, a neurologist solved the mystery. The impact to her skull had cut off certain pathways to her brain. She experienced temporary memory loss. It sometimes lasted hours—other times, days.

Ruby could read but couldn't write because she couldn't organize her thoughts logically. She had to quit her job at the Register. She went into therapy, knowing it would be a long time before she could have a normal life again. She was depressed about Nick's death and about my cutting her out of my life.

Kyle told me she was still living in the same place in Laguna Beach. Alone. All her friends had drifted away from her. She spoke to Kyle occasionally. Sometimes she forgot about the accident and asked about Nick and me. When she remembered, she cried.

I didn't sleep at all that night. I felt guilty about the way I had ignored Ruby. Was my guilt valid? I didn't know. I had to find out. The next morning, I rented a car and drove to Laguna Beach, to Ruby's home.

The spring rain fell constant and cold. To a visitor in a beach town, rain is a plus, as far as parking goes.

From the street where I parked, I could only see the old wooden fence and part of the roof.

Ruby's place used to be the garage of the white mansion down the hill. Even after the transformation to beach cottage it didn't have much square footage, but the view made you forget about "limited living space."

Ruby had always been a passionate gardener. She loved roses. The bushes looked like they hadn't been pruned in months, and the petals from the wilted flowers covered the brick path leading to the main entrance. I reached for the bell then remembered it had never worked. When I touched the door, it swung open. Music came from the back room, the one with the grand view.

My plastic raincoat made crinkly noises when I walked into the dark hallway. There was a musty smell, the smell of old beach houses on rainy days.

A melancholic solo from Miles Davis' trumpet welcomed me into the room.

She stood by the window, her back to the door.

I took a big breath. "Ruby."

Because of her neck brace, Ruby had to turn her entire body around in order to see me. She looked thinner than I remembered. Her hair was dull, with a few strands of gray visible near her scalp. Yet her eyes seemed as voracious as ever, her hunger insatiate. She opened her mouth but didn't say anything. She came over and gripped me in a hug so tight I could hardly breathe. She began to weep, saying my name over and over. "Lella, it's you. It's really you..."

"Watch it. You're getting my raincoat all wet." I swallowed the knot in my throat.

She stepped back, looking me over.

I smiled.

"Oh, you!" Then she started to cry again.

I cried too. She hadn't made it out of the accident without a scratch as I'd believed.

I moved in with Ruby. Kyle didn't approve but he kept his opinion to himself.

Neither Ruby nor I ever mentioned Nick.

I pruned her roses and ran errands with her, and she helped me look for a town house in Dana Point. By the time I closed escrow, Ruby was able to drive.

The day after I moved into my new place, she showed up at my door with a black kitten. Flash. It was a brand new beginning for each of us. That was four years ago. Four years of boring predictability. I would give anything to go back to that monotonous dullness, anything.

THIRTEEN

I sat at my kitchen table, eyes closed, searching for logic in this senseless situation. Shivers traveled through my body, but my hands burned hot against the cold glass of water and my mind's eye fought images of Kyle, Ruby and Larry.

Evening cloaked my home and my spirit. All my crying left me so drained I couldn't think straight. Poor Kyle. I couldn't bear to think about him in some dungeon-like, dangerous jail. I called the police department, trying to find out the address and the name of the detention place where Kyle was being held. Maybe I could call him, visit him, anything. Too soon, I was told, call back later. Between fits of desperation I phoned Bonnie's office, but reached a recording. Why did Kyle hire Bonnie? Larry's friend. How did Larry fit into this? Larry and Bonnie and the disposable phone I was instructed to answer. I had left the phone somewhere upstairs, and it was still there, unanswered. I kept the whole house dark and hoped by now even the most dedicated reporter would have given up and left.

The loud ring of the house phone startled me. I let the machine answer. "Damn it, Lella, I know you can hear me. Pick up the phone." Larry's voice was low and angry. I didn't move.

"Lella, I'm going to be at your front door in a minute. You can open the door or I'll let myself in. I don't want to attract attention, but if you don't care, we'll do it your way." A brief silence, then I heard the knob of my front door turn like magic. I jumped up and unlocked and yanked open the door. I wasn't going to give him the satisfaction of showing off his lock-picking skills. The outside lamp framed his silhouette, and I got a whiff of his aftershave when he came in.

"You can turn on the light. The reporters are gone.

There's a smash-up on Ortega Highway with some drunken celebrity. They'll be busy for a while."

I didn't move. We stood so close I felt his body heat, but it didn't warm my heart. He stepped away and went to turn on the dining-room chandelier. When the light hit, my swollen eyelids burned like open wounds. If he noticed he didn't acknowledge it.

"I brought you some food."

I didn't want his food; I wanted to hurt him the way I was hurting. All my troubles began with him. I had a perfectly ideal life and that perfect life had been blown apart the day he called about Ruby.

He stood by the dining-room table, studying me. I sensed it even though his face was shaded and I couldn't see his eyes. He wore the same jacket he had on when he drove me to meet his friend Bonnie. He pretty much looked the same way he did this morning, and if new emotions found their way into his soul, he concealed them well.

"I brought you some food," he repeated, and put a brown bag on the table. A bag with the Cannons logo on it.

He folded his jacket over the back of a dining chair then pulled out containers from the bag. My silence didn't seem to disturb him. Soon I saw a plate, silverware, butter and rolls on the table. I got curious, and he knew it. He took a step in my direction and gave me the slightest smile. "I didn't know what to get you so I brought the same food you ordered when we went there for dinner. It's still warm. I made sure." He remembered? Another step. He held out his hand and waited. I fought the urge to touch him, the urge to hide my sorrow against his heart. Feelings, old and not so old interwoven, sparring for control, announcing their power over me. No.

"You really should eat. Not eating isn't going to help." He spoke with the same tone of voice I used when Kyle was little and sick. I should have felt insulted, but at a deeper level I knew that such caring wasn't something Larry did often or randomly.

"I'm not going to eat, okay? You should go home."

"Lella, you may hold the key to Ruby's disappearance. You knew her better than anyone else. If she's out there, we'll find her, but you need to help."

I looked him in the eyes. "I want to talk to my son. Where is he?"

"I'm not sure where he's being held. He'll probably call you soon. He will call on your landline, collect. Make sure you answer. They aren't allowed much time and other inmates will be waiting to use the phones." A pause. "And every word gets recorded."

Someone knocked on the front door. I looked at Larry, not sure what to do. He put a finger on his lips. "Shhh."

We waited. His hand found mine on the table. The knocking grew louder.

"Ask who it is," he whispered in my ear. He got up and walked toward the door.

"Who is it?" I said.

"Mrs. York, it's me, Audrey. Your neighbor."

Larry turned his head, his eyes searching mine. I nodded yes, I knew her.

"Mrs. York, I heard about Kyle." She sounded concerned.

I hurried to open the door.

Audrey hesitated then came in. She looked at me, at my swollen face, and then at Larry. She shifted her weight from one foot to the other, like nervous people do. I had to introduce them and found myself mystified. Who was he going to be tonight? Larry the lover, Lieutenant Devin, Bonnie's friend or someone entirely different?

"I'm Larry Devin." He shook her hand, solving my dilemma, if only temporarily.

"I heard it on the news. They think Kyle did something to that friend of yours? The one who picked up your mail and fed your cat?"

I nodded. "I didn't know you met Ruby."

"She was very nice. I didn't talk to her until my aunt came over to visit. Well, she wasn't really our aunt. We called her Aunt Millie because she sometimes took care of us." She must have noticed the puzzled look on my face. "My brother and me."

"Where is David?"

"He's asleep. Tomorrow we need to get on the road very early. We're going back home for the funeral. Aunt Millie's funeral."

"I'm so sorry." The whole conversation felt unreal. Larry watched, pretending great interest.

"Her death was so unexpected. She drowned. It's so sad. One day she's here visiting, and a few days later they find her in the river." Audrey sounded crushed. Her eyes avoided mine. Tears glistened on her lashes.

"Did you live far away?" Larry's voice surprised us.

"We moved here from Parker, Arizona, after my dad was transferred. We still don't get to see him often, but I like to be near the beach."

Larry grasped my arm, moving closer, almost between Audrey and me.

"You say your Aunt Millie came to visit and met Ruby?" His voice had that calm charm he used on me when he asked me to dinner. What the hell was he up to?

"Yes. I had no idea Aunt Millie was coming, and we weren't home. Your friend—Ruby—kept her entertained until we got back. Apparently they had a lot in common. They were the same age and the same astrological sign. Aunt Millie believed very much in those sorts of things. A friend had given Aunt Millie a ride here, but she didn't have a ride back, so Ruby offered to take her home."

"To Parker?" I remembered what Kyle said about Ruby stopping to see him in Palm Springs. "She had gone to Parker to drop off something for Tom," he'd said. Maybe that was why she'd offered the aunt a ride? But Tom was already dead when she swapped the car in Palm Springs. None of this made sense.

"I'll have to leave you, ladies." Larry checked his watch. "I have an appointment with a friend and I'm running late. Nice meeting you, Audrey. Sorry about your loss." He turned to me. "Talk to you later. Answer your phone."

He must mean the phone Bonnie gave me, the one I hadn't answered. Then he left. I didn't want him to go, but didn't want him to know that I wanted him to stay.

"Audrey, I'm not sure what's going on with Ruby and Kyle." I paused to control the surge of hurt at the mention of my son's name. "Is there something I can do for you?"

"Not really." She was still standing by the door, doing the balancing trick with her feet. "Could you keep an eye on my place? I'll be back day after tomorrow. We're only spending one night up there. Maybe my dad can make it too. My dad is a commercial pilot. He was in England when I found out." She turned to leave. "Can you tell Kyle that I'm thinking of him?"

I nodded and she left. I locked the door behind Audrey and went to sit in the kitchen. Flash came out of nowhere, checking her empty food dish. I stroked her back, my mind still sorting out what just happened. Something Audrey said triggered a reaction in Larry. Suddenly he not only listened, but he asked questions. About Parker and the aunt. The aunt who drowned.

The house phone rang. I picked it up on the second ring and accepted the collect call with trembling hands and my voice quivering.

"Mom." Kyle's voice started the flood of tears again. "Mom, don't cry, please. We need to talk. I only have a few minutes. I didn't do it. Whatever they think I did to Ruby, it isn't true. I would never hurt her; you know that."

"I know, Kyle, I know. We must get you home. Why did you hire Bonnie?"

"I didn't hire Bonnie. I thought you did."

What? "When did you first talk to her?"

"When you saw me in court."

"Wait, didn't you ask for a lawyer when they arrested you?"

"Sort of. I tried to call you, but you weren't answering, and Carolyn was at that event waiting for me. It all happened so fast. The next thing I knew I was in a cell, and then in the morning I was in court."

"I need to get you a real lawyer."

"Bonnie isn't a lawyer?" He paused. "Mom, I've got to hang up or I'll get in trouble. These people don't kid around, Mom. Sorry, got to—" Click. Silence.

I forgot to ask what jail he was in. He didn't hire Bonnie. Larry had to be more involved in this mess than I first thought. But why? I felt manipulated, used.

All my pent-up emotions turned into anger. I grabbed the containers from Cannons and dumped them in the garbage. Too bad I couldn't do the same to the bearer. I hated the whole world. If only I could get my hands on Ruby. I wished the astrologer had been right. A dead woman would have not swapped cars with my son. Oh, God!

I turned off the lights and went upstairs to my bedroom, aware I wouldn't get much more sleep than the night before. I sat on the unmade bed. Should I take something to help me sleep? Tissues littered my bed from the previous hours of crying. Ruby's chart was among the tissues. I remembered something Audrey said about her aunt. "They had a lot in common, same age, same astrological sign." Mio dio. The Ponte Vecchio encounter flashed in my mind's eye in every detail. The only thing I gave to the astrologer was Ruby's birthdate and Los Angeles as the place of birth. No specific time, no details. Who knows how many baby girls could have been born that same day in LA County? Dozens. Hundreds! One of them could have been Audrey's aunt, the one who drowned. The chart of a dead woman could be the chart of any woman born the same day as Ruby. Why didn't I think of that before wasting time and energy over a stupid astrological chart, a worthless piece of paper? I tossed the tissues and the chart into the waste basket, then went to the bathroom to wash away my tears. Tonight I would sleep. Tomorrow I would fire Bonnie, hire a real lawyer and get Kyle home. I would not think about Larry, and I would find Ruby.

Flash hopped onto the bed, stretched and then settled next to me. I looked at my faithful pet. Here we were again, the two of us. I scooted closer to Flash and leaned over to turn off the light.

FOURTEEN

9:00 a.m. I stood in my kitchen, fully dressed. Already had my two cups of coffee and cherry yogurt. I fed the cat and was ready to go.

I took a deep breath and picked up the phone. Before I could punch in a single digit I heard a voice. "Good morning, Lella!"

What? I must have answered the phone before it had the chance to ring.

"Lella, it's Bonnie. How are you?" Ticked off and unprepared to speak to you? "I hear you want to fire me."

"Excuse me?"

"I spoke to Kyle. You can't fire me because you didn't hire me."

"Who hired you, and why?"

"Your son signed the retainer today. Larry 'hired' me originally. I assume out of guilt?"

"Guilt? About what?" Hundreds of thoughts fought in my mind for a chance to leap from my lips to her ear. Instead I sat, stunned by her statement. I let the silence build because I didn't know what to say.

"Lella, you need to trust me." She ignored my question. "I'll take good care of your son. I promise you."

"How is Kyle?" I attempted to head the conversation to a different direction in the hopes that Bonnie would forget my earlier question. I wasn't sure I could handle the answer.

"Not too happy about the situation, but he's getting a better understanding of how the system works and what we need to do to get him home."

I felt a surge of anger. If she was going to take care of Kyle, she would have made sure he didn't have to spend the night in jail. "When can I see him?"

"Late this morning. He is at the men's facility, very close to the courthouse where we were. You'll need identification. Don't bring anything of value inside with you. Dress modestly. No open-toed shoes. Lella, you must be strong. He's a good kid. Let's stick together and sort this mess out." She stopped talking, but somehow I knew she wasn't done. I heard her take a deep breath. "Did you talk to Larry?"

"About what?"

"About the missing woman, Ruby Russell. I understand you're best friends."

I hesitated. "I saw Larry last evening, but he was in a hurry." I avoided the Cannons details. "I guess we didn't get to talk about Ruby. What do you need to know?"

"I'll put together a list after I see Kyle. I'm expecting a complete police report."

She said goodbye. She didn't wait for me to answer her before she hung up on me.

I will not cry. I couldn't cry. Flash rubbed against my leg. She sensed my despair. I went upstairs and, like a mechanical doll, I changed from my suit to slacks and a sweater. Removed my jewelry, grabbed my purse, my car keys and out the door I went. I will not cry.

Driving always had a calming effect. Away from phone, television and distractions, I could sort out my thoughts and make sense of my often negative reasoning. Or I could have a good cry and feel renewed afterward.

Larry hired Bonnie to represent Kyle out of guilt. Guilt about what? Larry never met Kyle. Their paths never crossed. I needed to talk to Larry. I left the house feeling so stressed and confused that I couldn't remember if I put the cell phone in my purse. There was no way of pulling off the freeway. I didn't want to miss the visiting hours. I had no idea how long it would take me to find parking and fill out whatever forms were needed to get to see my son. The Larry puzzle would have to wait.

Much to my surprise, everything went well. The sheriff ran a smooth operation. Waiting for Kyle to get to the phone was the most painful part before the visit. I wasn't sure how I would react, how he would look or sound. The shuffling of his shackled feet when he exited the courtroom still tore my heart to pieces.

Then I saw him. He sat, and we looked at each other, separated by a thick glass. I was unable to reach over to touch him, to hold his hand. I wasn't even sure this was a private conversation. I remembered Larry's warning. "And every word gets recorded."

My brain knew it was my imagination, but my heart decided Kyle had lost weight overnight. We each picked up a phone.

"Hi, Mom." His voice didn't sound like his voice at all.

I swallowed my tears. The last thing Kyle needed was a weeping mother.

"Mom, what's up with you and Larry Devin?"

"What?" I felt my mouth open and stay that way, like a fish on a hook.

"Bonnie said your friend Larry is picking up the tab for my defense, and I'm sure it's not a small bill. Is he someone from the mission? A friend of Dad's?"

"No, no. Larry's a—retired detective...who..." I stopped short of saying "who won the lottery."

"Well, he is also a friend of Bonnie's. Maybe she's giving him a discount. Why do you want to keep Bonnie as your lawyer?" I asked.

"She came over last night after I called you. She isn't the type of lawyer who gets pushed around. Some of the guys, I mean the other, you know, prisoners"—I could see the embarrassment on his face when he mentioned anything related to the prison—"they must know who she is. They were high-fiving me, like I won the lottery." I blushed when he mentioned the lottery. Damn you, Larry Devin. I nodded my encouragement as he went on. "She stayed for over an hour. I understand much better what this is all about. It's just a matter of figuring out where Ruby is holed up with my Porsche, and I'm out of here."

I looked at him a long time. Was this my Kyle? I came here to comfort him, a ton of tissues in my pocket, and instead he was cheering me up. "Kyle, you are so right. Where can she possibly be? Certainly the police must be looking for her and your Porsche. Perhaps we can think about places she may be at and then we can compare notes? Do you have access to writing material? Should I go get you some?"

"Mom, that's a good idea. I have paper and a pencil, and I'll work on it. Do you think maybe she went back to Parker after she left Palm Springs with my car?"

We spent the last ten minutes analyzing more places Ruby was likely to be, but the big question was left unasked. Why? Why would Ruby put Kyle's life in jeopardy? Regardless of where she was, surely she must read the papers, listen to the radio and watch the news. Unless—the chart of a dead woman. Stop it.

"Mom, you don't need to hurry here to see me every day, really. I'm in a section for people who haven't gone to court yet, and it's not so bad. I'm a big boy, you know." He killed me and kept on smiling it was likely a ton wouldn't be nearly enough tissues.

Was Bonnie behind this? Not seeing him every day?

Visiting time was over, and Kyle was spared the paranoia burgeoning in my eyes–at least, that was what I figured he'd see if I stayed any longer.

⁓⁂⁓

Kyle was ready to fight this on his own, without my help, a side of him I hadn't discovered before. Then again, we hadn't shared much quality time together in the last few years. Sure, we exchanged weekly phone calls as generic as Sunday sermons. Now and then we would eat together on the run because Kyle always seemed to be stopping by on his way to here or from there. Somehow Mom's place was never the destination, only the quick stop in between. Dear God, what was happening to me? All these negative thoughts about my poor son. Like the old saying goes, it takes two to tango. The time Kyle managed to spend with me seemed to originate from a sense of duty, but I couldn't honestly say I did much to improve the relationship, perhaps because up till now, I hadn't suspected it could use improvement.

I couldn't remember the last time we did something spontaneous together, something just for the fun of it. Every mother-and-son activity was pre-planned and served a definite purpose always aimed at accomplishing a specific outcome. Often I would be asked to go to a movie premiere, in particular if Kyle's role was of a naive young family man. It made me feel important; it made me feel needed. Life just served me a slice of reality, a slice big enough to gag me.

Driving home after my visit with Kyle, it hit me that Flash was the only living being who needed me, because she couldn't get her bag of food out of the cupboard.

A sense of nothingness seized my brain, erasing the elation of my night with Larry, the illusion of my revamped sexuality. Once again, guilt prevailed. Had I been home, Kyle would have been able to reach me, and perhaps I could have kept him from spending time in jail. If my son and I were closer, I would have offered him my car for his business trip. I would have turned the Ferrari over to the police. That was what real mothers did. They took care of their children instead of cavorting with men they barely knew. I felt old, unwanted and unloved. A failure in every aspect of life.

All this mea culpa, mea culpa, mea maxima culpa meant nothing, of course. The more I beat myself up, the more I realized the real problem had little to do with the agonizing, Catholicism-induced guilt trip. All I needed was one person: Ruby. Find Ruby and force her to go the police and tell the truth. Voila. Simple. Problem solved.

What if I couldn't find Ruby?

Nonsense. Knowing Ruby, she was in some hotel with the stranger du jour, trying to fill the void left by Tom's death. She had a short attention span when it came to men. At some point she would come back home; she had to. Home? What home? She never spoke of relatives or good friends living outside California. If she drove Kyle's Porsche anywhere, she would attract attention. The police had the description, and this was no ordinary car. Of course, all this common sense was for my own benefit. I had to find something or someone to focus blame on before I lost my mind.

Ruby was that someone. And it appeared I was her only friend. Would she come knocking at my door?

I kept my speed under the limit. I didn't want to go home to my empty house. I could use a hug, a friendly voice, a shoulder to cry on. Maybe I should go to a busy shopping center, lose myself in the crowd. I had to face the truth: I had isolated myself. Ruby had been the main presence in my life outside of Kyle, and now here I was, alone. I wasn't about to call Larry. Stop thinking about Larry, and make yourself useful. Feed your cat.

I had been home for less than ten minutes when the phone rang.

"Hello."

"Lella, you're home." Larry's voice was full of relief. I, too, felt a wave of relief and other mixed emotions, but for different reasons than his, for sure. "You need to pack an overnight bag. I'll pick you up in a few hours."

I decided to play along. "Where are we going?"

"To my place." Over the phone came sounds of engines, traffic, horns blowing and brakes screeching. "Fucking idiots. Sorry about that. Truckers are racing with each other; they barely missed me."

"Where are you?" No sarcasm now.

"I'm on my way back from Parker."

Parker. He said Parker. Aunt Millie drowned in Parker. Audrey was in Parker. I remembered the way he spoke to her the night before, with a super-sized helping of charm, and how quickly he left without even a good-night kiss. I remembered Bonnie's statement about his guilt.

I hung up. My hands shook. The phone rang again before I reached the far end of the room. I couldn't ignore it. It might be Kyle, and it was his only means of communication.

I lifted the phone to my ear without speaking because my anger had reached the point of eruption.

"Lella?" Bonnie. "Lella, are you there? Can you hear me?"

"Yes, Bonnie, I'm here. I can hear you." What now?

"Hey, what's wrong?"

"Nothing's wrong. Why are you calling? Is it about Kyle?"

"Did you talk to Larry?" She ignored my questions.

"Okay, you know what? This is stopping right here, right now. What? Are the two of you tag-teaming me? What is it you want from me? The only precious thing in my life is sitting in a prison, and you're supposed to be the genius getting him out. Why aren't you there with Kyle?" I sounded shrill and out of control, even to myself.

"Remember I mentioned a list of questions I'd have for you after talking to Kyle? Well, I have that list." She spoke with the same silky voice she might use to reason with a child throwing a tantrum.

I took a long breath and mentally counted to ten. "Fine, Bonnie. Ask away."

"Actually, I'd prefer to meet with you and talk about it over a cup of coffee."

My suspicion resurfaced. Talk about it over a cup of coffee? What was it with these people? They had nothing to do but chit-chat all day?

"Lella?"

"I'm thinking."

"Stop thinking. I'm coming over and we can talk."

"What do you mean you're coming over? To my house?"

"Yes, I'll be there in twenty-five minutes. I'm coming straight from seeing Kyle. See you." Click.

No, you aren't. She was lying. I knew it. I sensed it. She wasn't coming from the jail. Something was up. First Larry wanted me to pack and go with him, and now Bonnie was on her way here. They want something from me. What?

Bonnie said she'd be here in twenty-five minutes? Okay, I could be gone in ten. All the pent-up anger and guilt I brought with me from Kyle's visit fueled my sense of rebellion.

I went upstairs. Flash followed me, possibly surprised by my misguided burst of energy. I was practically running. This time I wasn't going to forget my phone. I threw some clothes and toiletries in a large canvas bag without paying much attention at first. When I packed two unmatched shoes, I stopped.

What was I doing? Running away? I couldn't run away from myself. I emptied the bag on the unmade bed, grabbed my overnight luggage and started to repack, this time like I meant it. I would spend the night in LA, at Kyle's condo. I had a key. What if Ruby was hiding at his place? Oh, my God! I felt like I'd found the answer to all our problems.

"Okay, Flash, you be good, I'm leaving enough food for you until I get back. I need to clear my mind and go check out Kyle's place. Just in case. And I'll make sure no food is getting spoiled, and no plants are dying of thirst. Try not to miss me."

Flash kept on cleaning herself, unconcerned by my monologue.

I double checked doors and windows and left a light on in the laundry room for Flash. Good, I still had ten minutes on Bonnie. Bag on my shoulder, carry-on in hand, I opened the front door wide and found myself staring at two men in dark suits.

Jehovah's Witnesses? Who let them through the gate? Then I noticed two more people in uniform behind them, carrying tool boxes?

"Mrs. York?" A tall man in a suit.

He knew my name? I stood there, my mind blank.

"Are you Donatella York?" His voice was businesslike, yet friendly. Not intimidating. The sheer number of strangers standing around staring did the trick anyway.

"Yes, that's me." Behind me, my door was wide open. I swallowed air. My heart pounded so hard I thought the neighbors next door could hear it, except they were in Parker, Arizona. Snap out of it.

"Who are you? What's this about? I'm in a hurry." Breathe, Lella, breathe.

The tall man fanned a tri-folded piece of paper. It looked official.

"Hello, boys. Let me guess—it's a search warrant." Bonnie's cheerful voice came from somewhere behind the growing crowd of suits and uniforms outside my front door. Oh, Bonnie.

The tall man, still holding the white paper, broke into a wide, genuine smile. "If it isn't my favorite lawyer." He tilted his head in her direction." We need to stop meeting this way."

Bonnie grabbed the paper from him. "Always disrupting my clients' peaceful lives." They appeared to know each other so well, it all sounded like a familiar game.

"Lella, why don't you wait for me in the car?" She handed me her car keys. I was still sucking air. "It's okay, Lella. I'll explain it to you. You can leave your bags here."

The kaleidoscope of emotions twirling inside my head must have been obvious because she said, "It's to help Kyle. Go to the car. I'll be there in a minute."

FIFTEEN

"Okay, Bonnie, here we are, in your car. Start talking. What was that all about? An army of cops invading my house, without warning. I'm a suspect now? Suspected of doing what?"

"I understand how it would look to you, Lella. No, you are a not a suspect. It's quite the opposite. The detectives are trying to establish a timeline, I'm sure. If Kyle is telling the truth, this can only help him."

"I'm beginning to think you're using my son as the bait to get me to go along with all this hush-hush nonsense. Timeline? I was out of the country and my son was in Palm Springs. Somebody is fudging the truth, and it isn't us."

"Again, no one is accusing you of anything. It will all be clear very soon, I promise. It takes time. We are all fighting for the same cause, to get Kyle home."

By the time Bonnie parked her car at the Dana Point harbor and we found a shaded bench to sit on, I was done with the rant, the threats and the begging. Now, feeling useless and deflated, I appeased myself by staring at the frothy waves splashing against the rocks below.

"Do you think Ruby is hidden in one of my closets and I forgot to tell the cops? I haven't seen her since the day I left for Europe, over a month ago. She's probably in some hotel in Vegas, gambling away poor Tom's money and driving Kyle's car." I said "poor Tom," like Mrs. Snoopy. Oh, mio dio.

"They know that. The detectives aren't concerned with you. They want to make sure no clues are missed. In the end, it will help Kyle—if everything he told the police checks out."

We'd danced around the ifs and the maybes so many

times I'd run out of new steps. Aside from that, I felt terrible for allowing Larry to distract me from my son.

"Larry should be back before sundown."

Damn it, here we go again. She knows what I'm thinking.

"You know about the trip?" That sounded innocent enough—no jealousy, no anger.

She tilted her head so that we faced each other. "Of course I know about it. Why?"

"You two must be really close friends."

"Friends? Oh, we're a lot more than friends."

That was not the answer I needed to hear. I rested my chin into my hands and looked at the ground. The last thing I wanted was for Bonnie to guess my thoughts.

"I wouldn't be sitting here with you right now if it hadn't been for Larry." Her voice was trancelike; even her expression reflected an altered state of mind.

I felt uncomfortable, like I'd been caught reading someone else's diary. I missed the security of my home. My home? It was probably being violated in more ways than there were ants on the ground. I kept quiet. I wanted to grasp the underlying meaning of Bonnie's one-way conversation. Maybe it was a confession, a way of freeing herself from guilt. Or maybe I was reading too much into it.

"We've known each other for over twenty years. We met at Parents Without Partners."

"You have children?"

"Had. They are not children anymore." Bonnie's voice was brisk enough to discourage any question. She put her hand on her forehead like a visor, but the sun wasn't very bright. She rubbed her temples—would the motion help her remember? Or forget? "Larry was a big hit as you can imagine. One daddy to a dozen or so of us mommies. The odds were in his favor. And what a daddy he was—young, good looking, caring, yada, yada, yada. He had temporary custody of Olivia, his precious little girl, while the mother was out of the country on a fundraising assignment for the non-profit she worked for."

Daddy and mommies? Yada, yada, yada? The Bonnie sitting next to me on the bench had little in common with Bonnie the lawyer. I wished I could get up, walk away, turn back time, to before I met Bonnie, and Larry. Oh, Larry.

"He made it his mission to bring joy to as many of us as possible." She sounded amused by the implication of his multiple romances. "He managed to do it without causing jealousy or competition among us. The man was gifted that way." She smiled. Were the memories of the indiscretions the reason for the smile? "There was only one problem. He still lived with his mother here, in Dana Point." Larry lived with his mother, here in Dana Point?

"So the sex was always at the woman's house or in a hotel room. And that was how Mr. Devin happened to save my life." She stopped talking, let her hand drop to her lap and kept her eyes on that distant horizon and the sun lowering into the Pacific. I wanted to say something, but the knot in my throat wasn't budging. This woman sitting next to me was telling me about her affair with the man I considered my lover and, oddly enough, instead of feeling resentment, I felt compassion. I wanted to put my arms around her and tell her everything was going to be okay.

"I was so broke, just out of law school." A big sigh. "A single mother of twin boys. I lived in this one-room apartment over a friend's garage. Olivia's mother was due back soon, and I knew if I didn't connect with Larry right then, I'd never see him again. I found an excuse to get him to my place after he got off work. He knew the score. We did some necking in the back of the car before, but I wanted more. I spent my last few dollars on a six-pack of beer, got a friend to take the twins for the night, and I waited, and I waited. He never showed up. My phone had been disconnected because I was too broke to pay the bill, and I didn't want to walk to the corner phone in case I missed him." She stopped talking, her eyes fixed straight ahead. I didn't know what to say or what to do.

Part of me wanted to disappear, but the other part was anxious to hear the end of the story. There had to be an end. "I had some over-the-counter sleeping pills. I popped a few to dull the pain. I drank a beer. I repeated the process a few times. Next thing I remember, I woke up in Larry's house, with his mother, a nurse, watching over me. He was late coming to my place because he had to work overtime and didn't know how to get in touch with me. By the time he got there, I'd passed out. The man knew if this showed up on my record my professional career would be over before it ever started. His mother called in some favors. They kept me out of the emergency room and still saved my life and my future. That's way beyond friendship." She stood and stretched her arms.

I guessed she considered the discussion over and done with. That was not the way I saw it. My mind spun with questions. What happened after that? Did they have an affair? How long did it last? Where were her twins now?

"I'm getting cold and hungry. Let's go get something. There's a nice coffee house at the south end." She looked at me, waiting for an answer.

I shrugged. "You're my ride home." That was all I could say without sounding angry and resentful, and I felt a little of both. I had planned to visit Kyle on my way to his condo. What if he called while the detectives, or whatever these cops are called, were there searching?

"Bonnie, where are they searching? Like, my living room? Where?"

"Everywhere they want, dear."

"Even my bedroom?"

"Even your bedroom." She nodded.

"What are they searching for?"

"Anything and everything." She shrugged.

It was that time of the evening when the sun sets and

light and darkness mingle. They blend like milk and coffee in a cappuccino. A mild smell of decaying fish rose from the jetties, and few crafts sailed close to shore. We walked toward the southern end of the harbor where in late spring tourists wait for the boats that take them out whale watching. I had run out of neutral subjects to talk about. Apparently, so did Bonnie. Lights came on around us. Cannons Restaurant, high on the hill, looked like a ball of fire, the last rays of sun reflecting on its glass facade.

I was up there with Larry less than ten days ago, yet it seemed like a long time had passed.

"It's getting cold." Bonnie turned to me. "If I feel cold with my extra padding, you must be freezing." She smiled. "Let's get back to the car and go see what the boys are doing."

I knew she meant the detectives at my place. I nodded and we turned to walk back to the parking lot.

<hr/>

From outside my house you couldn't guess someone was inside going through all my things. The front door wasn't locked. I pushed it open. Bonnie stood on the threshold. Before I could call out, the tall detective appeared, followed by the other three. They had several small bags of stuff. I wanted to see what they were taking.

"Perfect timing." The tall man noticed Bonnie by the door. She nodded.

"What did you take? What's in the bags?" The pitch of my voice sounded a little crazy. I felt a lot crazier. Bonnie laid her hand on my arm. If it was meant to reassure me, it wasn't working. The tall man had something for me to sign, and he wanted me to get swabbed.

"Swab? Me? What for?" The outrage was real. On TV they only swabbed criminals or suspected criminals. What was happening?

Bonnie stepped in. "I'll take care of this. Lella, this is to eliminate your DNA from any other. It's pretty standard.

Trust me." Trust me. Here we go again. I'm supposed to trust the whole world, the same world that trusts no one.

Then the man swabbed me. The other three looked uncomfortable, ready to go. Bonnie read the document he'd given her. She looked at the paper, then at the detective. She handed me a pen and pointed to the bottom of the page. "Here, sign." She sensed my resistance. "It's okay. You're acknowledging what they're removing, what's in the bag. It's a receipt, in a way. You'll get everything back...eventually." She looked at the tall man. His expression didn't change. I wanted them out of my house. The sentiment must have been mutual. As soon as I signed, they lined up and marched out, bags, tool boxes and all. Bonnie went to close the door behind them.

"Let's sit down and look through the list together. Not bad, not bad at all."

"Bonnie, what are you talking about?" I had problems dealing with the situation. I had to know what the cops collected from my house. It was my right. "If I'm not a suspect, why are they taking my stuff?"

"Relax, not much stuff taken. A bar of soap from the guest bath? That's a new one. And—"

"Wait, wait, they removed a bar of soap? Yeah, the better to wash their mouths out."

"Not funny." Bonnie's voice and attitude changed. "Damn it."

"What? What is it?" I found myself frightened, without knowing why.

"Where did you leave the disposable phone we gave you?"

"Somewhere in my bedroom. I never used it."

She turned to look at me. That old cliché "if looks could kill" floated through my head. Bonnie took a long, slow breath and the fire from her eyes subsided, sort of.

"You may not have used it, but I left a few messages and I'm wondering what there is on that phone from Larry. He'll be crucified over this." She kept avoiding my glance and shaking her head. I didn't have a clue what she meant. So I did what any Italian does under similar circumstances.

"Bonnie, how about I fix us some dinner?"

She kept shaking her head and then sighed. "Larry will have to deal with it. Let's go take a look at this guest bath. See why our friends found it so interesting."

We climbed the stairs to the bathroom. "That bath hasn't been used for months. Kyle didn't have time to take a shower the other day. He was in and out and then got arrested. I'm guessing it was the same soap that was there before I left for Italy. I have extra bars." I realized how stupid all this chatter sounded. I switched on the light. The bathroom looked exactly the way it always did. The missing bar of soap was the one by the double sinks.

"Lella, when you came back from overseas, was anything different?'

"In here? No, not really. Wait. Yes, the toilet paper. Ruby must have run out of toilet paper and for some reason decided to buy more. So silly, I have plenty of toilet paper in the other bath. She replaced it with a different brand. I noticed and was going to ask Ruby about it."

"Anything else?"

"No, of course not. The rug was a little damp. Maybe Flash had an accident and Ruby used the toilet paper to clean up. I don't know. I'm sure it's dry by now. Why all this sudden interest about a bathroom?"

"Precisely what I was thinking. Lella, can you show me exactly where the wet spot was?"

"It wasn't wet, just a little damp. Here." I put my foot on the carpet, in proximity to the bathtub, and then looked at Bonnie.

She got down on her knees, just like I did that evening. She ran her hands all over the rug, fast, her face close to the rug, smelling it. I could feel the intensity of her action.

"Nothing was missing? You're sure?"

Her questions had gone from curious to just plain annoying. My stomach growled. I'd had so little food in the last few days, I felt lightheaded. "Nothing. Bonnie, it's not like I keep a list of bathroom items. I mean, I live alone. What? Someone is going to break in to steal my toilet paper?"

Did she pick up the annoyance in my voice? She stood, pulled her sweater down to cover her hips and said, "If you don't mind, I'd like to take the list with me to make a copy. Unless you have a fax in the house. We could fax it to my office. I need to get going."

For the first time since the cops arrived at my front door, I realized Bonnie had spent the whole afternoon and evening with me, listening to my complaints, justified or not. If she billed by the hour, I owed her a lot more than I could afford. "Are you sure I can't get you something to eat before you drive back? It's a long ride. It wouldn't take much time, maybe a sandwich?"

"No, thanks. I'll chew gum. It helps me process information while I drive." That made a lot of sense, so I walked her to the door and said goodbye.

"Lock your door." Then she left.

I did.

SIXTEEN

I overslept. Not by choice. The minute I swallowed the sleeping pill I knew I'd made a mistake. The effects would linger into the morning. I slept ten hours straight, and while my face looked rested, my brain was full of chaotic thoughts. By the time I showered and went downstairs to get the daily paper from my front door, it was close to 10:00 a.m.

Lucky for me, Kyle called before I went to bed, so I didn't have to worry about missing him. He sounded a lot more together.

"Carolyn visited with great news." The story of his arrest had created a buzz in the entertainment industry. I didn't want to burst his bubble by reminding him that making the news from jail was hardly something to brag about it, but I was no expert on the subject. I told him about the search warrant, and he said his place had been searched, but nothing removed. The fact that he hadn't been home for about six weeks was probably factored in. His laptop was in the Ferrari when they arrested him. God knows he kept everything, important or trivial, in that piece of electronic wonder. That bit of news put an end to my theory of Ruby hiding out in his condo.

I went to get the newspaper and felt warm and tubby in my shocking pink chenille robe, shuffling my fuzzy pink slippers with rhinestone initials—Kyle's version of Christmas glam for Mom. Flash had acted restless since I got out of bed, probably because she wasn't used to my sleeping in. The minute I opened the door and bent over to pick up the paper, she bolted and was gone. Shoot. I was in no mood to chase a mercurial cat. She could find her way home when she was ready to come back.

I noticed the brown slip-on first. I knew without

looking up whose feet these were. No. Why me? Why now? I couldn't spend the rest of my morning hunched over, on the threshold of my house. I had to get up, do something.

"Good morning, Lella. How are you today?" Blood rushed to my head when I straightened myself a little too fast. Larry stood in front of me, all smiles, a matching Styrofoam cup of coffee in each hand. He seemed amused by how scarlet my cheeks turned, and was not doing much to hide it either. He handed me a coffee and I robotically took it. He placed his free hand under my chin, tilted my face up and kissed me softly. Ah, the temptation to dump my cup on his head. I closed my eyes and counted to ten, or at least tried to.

Voices came from the path leading to the guest parking. Voices and cops. The tall, dark suit from yesterday walked toward my place. A female with short hair and a cute face trotted next to him, attempting to keep up with his pace. They were at my front door before I could count to seven.

"Hey, Devin, what's up?" Yesterday's cop patted Larry on the shoulder. They were about the same height and obviously knew each other. He then turned and smiled at me, in my silly, juvenile bathrobe, a smile that told me he knew things about me today that he didn't know yesterday. I felt more heat reaching my face. I glanced at the young woman and found that same smile, a smile full of unspoken awareness. I wondered if they saw Larry kissing me. This was so awkward, so embarrassing. Why must I be in a bathrobe and rhinestone slippers, so late in the day? What were they all thinking?

Larry addressed the woman. "Morning, Florian." He sipped from his cup. "Is Bob treating you right?"

"You know he is, and if he wasn't, would I be telling?" She had nice teeth, and when she smiled little wrinkles formed just above the bridge of her nose. Now that we were close, she wasn't as young as I thought. "We miss you, though," she added, winking at Larry.

"Let's go in." Larry put his hand on my elbow and coaxed me inside. He acted as if he'd expected these two to show up, and his body language left no doubt about our degree of familiarity. I felt clueless and nervous—pretty much the same way I'd be feeling ever since I came back from Italy.

"Hummm." I cleared my throat. "I—how about someone tells me what's going on?"

"Sorry, Mrs. York, we should have phoned." Bob looked at Larry, and I had the feeling he was counting on Larry to say something. That didn't happen, so Bob spoke to me again. "It's about the bathroom. We understand something was missing when you came back from your trip."

Bonnie? Bonnie told them about our conversation? Why? Whose side was she on anyway? "Nothing was missing." I found it hard to talk around the sense of outrage flooding my brain. "The toilet paper had been replaced. Maybe Ruby ran out of it and didn't know I kept extra in my own bathroom. Not a big deal."

"Was it just one roll? A package of four? Do you know?"

"It was a pack of four, generic brand, one ply, white. Anything else?"

Larry moved closer to me and put his hand on the small of my back. "Lella, it's okay. Why don't you show Bob the toilet paper? Would that be better?" I wasn't sure who he was talking to, but I found myself nodding and moving toward the stairs while seething inside. Larry and Bob followed.

"No one has used that bathroom since I've been back." I held up my robe, which was now dragging on the stairs. "I mean, no one was here and Kyle was in and out, so aside from Flash and me—"

"Who's Flash?" Detective Bob asked.

"My cat." We stood in the bathroom. I pointed to the roll on the paper holder, went to the small closet and handed him the pack with three rolls in it. He accepted with some hesitation. Maybe he should have been wearing rubber gloves. Incompetent. I almost said it out loud.

"Can you think of anything else, Mrs. York?"

"No, but you're welcome to look around. I'm going to get dressed. I'll be right back, gentlemen." Finally, I had my brain back.

I walked away and overheard Larry say, "She's Italian." He sounded pretty pleased with that statement. I wasn't sure if it was because he'd never met an Italian woman before or if he liked Italians in general. Either way, I decided to take it as a compliment.

I pulled on some knit pants and a long-sleeved T-shirt and went right back downstairs. The three of them were chatting. I decided to play along. "How about some coffee?" I offered. I had forgotten about the coffee Larry brought.

Bob shook his head. "No, thanks, we should be going."

"Mrs. York, are you into the metaphysical?" Florian addressed me. I looked at her a little puzzled. I had no idea what she meant.

"The metaphysical? You mean like talking to the dead or something?"

"No, I was thinking more about tarot cards."

"I like astrology." Visions of the chart of the dead woman flashed in my mind's eye. Then I got it. "You found Ruby's chart?"

A big smile lit Florian's face. "Yes."

"I had it done in Florence, the last day I was there. It was going to be a surprise, a present for her. A chart handwritten. In Italy. How did you know?"

"It was in your trash." She spoke in a low voice, apologetic. "It was part of the things we removed yesterday."

"Mrs. York." Bob's voice came from behind me. "We thought you were into Satanic rituals, but Florian here figured it out right away." He didn't sound amused. Neither was I.

I turned to look at Larry, hoping to get his reaction to

all this, but just then something peculiar happened.

A soft bing. No, two separate, yet similar bings. A buzzing and two bings. Three hands grabbed for cell phones and three pairs of eyes looked at them. It was so perfectly timed, it seemed rehearsed. Florian reacted first. She let out a happy "Yes!" and raised her fist holding the cell phone. Larry and Bob high-fived each other. And me? I stood there looking at them as stumped as before, but at least now I had clothes on.

This was the kind of scene you see in the movies, brotherhood or fraternity, or something, of the police force. All for one, one for all? These people were celebrating, but what? The fact that Larry wasn't even an active detective didn't seem to matter, they were in this together. I felt invisible.

"This changes things." Florian smiled.

"What changes what things?" I asked.

The three of them exchanged glances. Larry finally spoke. "I'm walking them to the car. I'll be right back and explain." I watched them quickly step out the door. Simply by habit, I locked it behind them.

While I waited for Larry to come back, I mentally listed questions I must ask him. I would start with wanting to know about the guilty remark Bonnie made. Followed by what just happened. Then we would move on to the trip to Parker. The coffee he brought me was still there, untouched and now cold. My first impulse was to dump it in the kitchen sink, but bringing coffee after I hung up on him the day before was a nice gesture. I poured it into my favorite mug, added some milk and put it in the microwave.

It was almost noon, Flash had skulked back and was licking her paws on the kitchen floor, and my stomach growled. I decided to have some peanut butter on toast. All my plans were sinking. I wanted to go visit Kyle after I went to the Return of the Swallows planning meeting at the mission, and then there was Larry and getting to the bottom of what he knew. I toasted the bread, spread peanut butter on it. By the time I was done munching it became apparent that Larry wasn't coming back. I looked around. He'd left behind the empty Styrofoam cup and a list of unanswered questions. Damn him, anyway.

SEVENTEEN

All the peanut butter and toast in the world couldn't fill the emptiness at the pit of my stomach. I went upstairs to ease the tension and to stop listening for Larry's footsteps.

I sat on my custom-made bed in my girly bedroom with a view of the ocean and asked myself, "Is this it? Is this the preview of things to come? Will I be spending the rest of my life waiting on a man? I am not going to fall into that trap again, never."

What I felt for Larry was so different from what I had with Nick. Not because I was married to Nick. Our relationship had always been more stable, and even in times of conflict we could find common ground with neither of us ending up emotionally bloody. Plus, over the years I learned to let things go, look the other way; it made life easier.

Larry, with his unreadable eyes. Larry, with the laissez faire of a Swiss guard. Larry, who lit the bonfire of passion when I had resigned myself to a life of celibacy.

Was this fiery turmoil an age thing? How would I know? Underneath the battered ego, I wanted him so bad I would run to him if he called out to me.

The phone rang and hope crashed the gate of my self-control. "Yes?" I sounded hoarse, even to myself.

"Lella? Are you okay?" Sabrina, from the mission.

"Yes, sure." I cleared my throat. "I'm fine, and I didn't forget about the meeting."

"About the meeting." It was Sabrina's turn to clear her throat. "We were thinking, you know, with your son and all that's going on..." She paused, and I didn't like where she was going.

"We? Care to tell me who we is?" That didn't sound grammatically correct, but grammar wasn't high on my list.

"The committee. It's because of all that publicity about Kyle. If you're at the mission, the media will be after you instead of the swallows."

"The invisible swallows?" Why did I say that? A good docent never mentions the fact that the swallows stopped coming back to the mission years ago. "Never mind, I get it. I'm persona non grata. Thanks a lot. I've been a volunteer for nearly ten years, and this is the thanks I get. Have a good Fiesta de Las Golondrinas." I hung up. Misplaced anger? Maybe.

I felt sick. Mad as hell and sick. Never mind that given a chance to visit Kyle over the meeting, I would have canceled the meeting without a bit of guilt. That was not the point. I splashed my face with cold water, hoping it would help. I turned off the faucet and heard what seemed to be a pounding sound. I stood still and listened. Maybe it was someone working outside. No, I heard it again, louder. It came from downstairs. I didn't know what to do. I grabbed my phone; I figured I could always call 911.

Call 911? Crazy, I was losing my mind. Halfway down the stairs I heard the thumping and this time I had no doubt; someone was pounding on my front door.

All the pent-up anger and disappointment must have fueled my arm's strength, because the way I opened it, the door slammed against the side wall.

Larry looked at me, and I sensed curiosity in his eyes. "Hello. Are you that happy to see me or is it a caffeine overdose?" He sounded cheerful. Did he know he'd been gone for over forty-five minutes? His calm and pleased attitude made me feel petty and small. Maybe he was a great guy and I was a demanding bitch.

"Wait." He stood on the threshold. "You thought I left, didn't you? Was I gone that long?" He put his hand under my chin like before, but instead of kissing me, he forced me to look him in the eyes. "You are angry. What? You thought I drove all the way here to deliver coffee?" No more cheerfulness in his voice.

I kept quiet, observing his eyes narrowing, a furrow forming on his forehead. I could almost hear the wheels in his brain turning. He was getting closer to the ugly truth, and I had no place to hide that cloud of suspicion I carried with me like a second shadow. I felt his fingers under my chin release.

He knew. He took a step back and stood outside my door. The expression on his face wasn't one of triumph for outing my mistrust, nor of anger for my judging him. I read sadness and thought, He's leaving. He isn't going to stick around to find out why I thought that he left. Panic filled my heart and my brain. I didn't want him to see it, and there we stood, without speaking, without touching.

The midday sun over us burned my eyes when I looked up, so I couldn't see his face anymore. I watched him move toward the door, hesitant at first, then he stepped over the threshold and put his arms around me and held my face against him. All I could think was that a lot more than a threshold was crossed.

We stood entwined, inhaling each other's familiar scents, processing our thoughts. Aroused and aware of each other's desire, but as if by unspoken consent, not acting on it.

Larry spoke first. "I didn't know Bob and Florian were going to show up at your house. And I did end up talking shop, letting time slip away. However, seems to me there's a lot more brewing in your head for you to react that way to such a simple situation." He let go of me and his lips brushed my hair. "Let's talk about this."

I felt so overwhelmed by his willingness to salvage whatever we had between us that I would have gladly forgotten about my list of important questions. Why can't relationships come with an instruction manual for unsophisticated adults like me?

We sat on the sofa, close, but not too close. "Why did

you hire Bonnie to represent Kyle?" I really wanted to ask, "Why are you paying Bonnie's fees?" but this sounded less accusatory. It wasn't a question he expected, I could tell.

"Bonnie? It's not a big deal. I'm always doing favors for her clients. It's payback time." His voice cheerful again.

I would have accepted that had it not been for that "guilty" word that Bonnie had dropped on me so strategically.

"Bonnie said you hired her." I swallowed hard. "Because of guilt." There, it was out there. Ball's in your court, Larry.

He cocked his head and looked at me, his eyes aloof. Nothing on his face flinched. We hadn't moved an inch, yet the distance between us grew. I'm not sure how long we stayed that way. All was quiet in the house, the deceptive quiet of a prison yard. He stood, walked to the patio door and glanced at the small garden. I couldn't see his face.

"Guilt is not something I experience often. I do what I have to do and that's it. If consequences arise, I handle them." He turned to look at me, his back to the glass door.

"Okay," I heard myself say.

"I called in the Ferrari."

I didn't have a clue what he was talking about. My ignorance must have showed on my face. He shook his head and ran his fingers through his hair. He was nervous, a break in the steel armor.

"That's how your son got picked up. Because I called in the missing car." I felt my eyes dilate, like they were about to pop off their sockets. He noticed it too, and the rest of the words came rushing out. "Lella, I had no idea he was driving the car. We—the police—were looking for a Ferrari with Ruby Russell at the wheel. I was being a cop." He seemed to wait for my reaction.

I rested my back against the pillows, closed my eyes so he couldn't read them and tried to comprehend what he just told me. The saddest part was that somehow I was glad, glad about the car, glad that it had nothing to do with Parker and Audrey. Glad that he had my son arrested? I was being a cop. Bad answer. But I knew it was true. He had no idea about Kyle and the Ferrari. I didn't even know anything until a few hours before the arrest—and I'm the mother and best friend. Once again, Ruby was the center of the mess. Larry stood, waiting for me to say something. I liked that sense of power. A whole new feeling.

"Can you please sit down? You're making me nervous. Sit down and tell me the full story. I need to get a better idea of the sequence."

He sat on the same spot as before. A strand of hair fell on his forehead, and I fought the urge to push it back. "I was coming off the 5 and had to go under the freeway to get to your place, and I saw the Ferrari entering the ramp to the north. I had just heard that it was listed as missing. I didn't see the license plate, but there aren't that many Ferraris. Plus, I figured Ruby was coming from your house." He waited for me to say something. His logic was flawless, but I wasn't about to tell him that. "When I picked you up you didn't mention Ruby visiting you, and frankly, at that point, I had other things on my mind. I forgot about the Ferrari until the next morning." I sensed his nervousness. I wanted to hug him and hated myself for it.

"I woke early, but didn't want to wake you. You slept so peacefully." He looked straight into my eyes, and I felt heat rush into my cheeks—so much for my sense of power. "I went into my office. My computer feeds info twenty-four seven and there it was, Kyle York arrested driving stolen car. Still I didn't make the connection. Out of curiosity I called one of my buddies on duty. When he gave me the news, it finally hit me how the whole thing would play out to an outsider. Cop gets kid arrested and then sleeps with the mother? That's where the guilt kicked in, I guess. I didn't want you to get hurt. My next call was to wake up Bonnie." Again, he waited. "I can fire her if that's what you want."

He would fire Bonnie if I wanted.

Larry Devin was a nice man. He was also a cop. I seemed to be helplessly in love with him. In a sense it was lucky that Larry called the Ferrari in. Now I was thinking like a cop. I shook my head, scooted over a little and put my hand in Larry's.

"Lella, about the car."

"Shhh."

"We have it. Kyle's Porsche was located this morning."

"What?"

"Remember when our phones went off at the same time? That was it."

"Oh my God. They found the Porsche. Is Ruby okay?"

He looked at me as if I spoke in tongues. "Ruby? No, no trace of Ruby."

EIGHTEEN

Kyle's smile lifted my spirits. I was visiting my son in jail in the middle of the afternoon, and it was okay. Sort of going with the flow, accepting reality. I picked up the phone, aware of Kyle glancing at Larry.

"Mom." The excitement in his voice, pure joy to my heart. "Did you hear about my Porsche?"

He said my Porsche—good.

"I did, Kyle, I did. Well, maybe our idea about Ruby hiding at your place wasn't so far-fetched, but if she ever was there, she'd be long gone now."

He nodded, still looking excited.

"Listen, I'd like you to meet someone." I turned to Larry and he moved closer. "Kyle, this is Larry Devin." I waited.

The only reaction from my son was an even wider smile. I handed the phone to Larry and stepped back. We had discussed all this on the drive up from my house. Larry had questions regarding the Porsche, and I figured I might as well introduce the two of them.

"Hi, Kyle."

"Nice to meet you sir, and thank you so much for sending Ms. Bonnie." My son, the prince of politeness.

"Call me Larry; it will be easier on both of us." I watched him readjust himself on the chair and move closer to the glass divider. "I'm checking information for your lawyer, Ms. Bonnie. And we wondered if you have any idea which way Ruby went when she left your hotel room to get the Porsche?"

"Actually, I was asleep. I overslept and was late on the set. I felt tired and dragged all day long. Ruby's whole visit is kind of foggy." He paused. "So, will I be getting out now that they've found my car? It's obvious that Ruby is alive and well."

"How so?"

"How else could the car get there? In my parking space, in my condo building? The police had already searched my place. They knew the car wasn't there a few days ago, and I've been locked up the whole time since."

"Too bad there aren't any surveillance cameras in that building of yours—would have made things easier. They're checking the car for fingerprints and other evidence that may help to establish how the vehicle got there."

"Will it take long?" Kyle looked so vulnerable and full of hope.

"It's hard to tell because it's out of our jurisdiction. You live in Los Angeles. This is Orange County. Each department works a little differently. The fact that they've already gone through your condo once will make it easier and quicker." Larry glanced at me. "I'll let you talk to your mom. If somewhere down the line you feel like talking to me, don't hesitate to tell Bonnie. We're old friends."

I was happy about the last statement. Hopefully Kyle wouldn't ask me too many details about my acquaintance with Larry, at least not now with all the excitement in the air.

"Kyle, when I visited you before, I forgot to tell you about Audrey. Her aunt in Parker died and she had to go to the funeral with her little brother. She asked me to explain and tell you she's thinking about you."

"Oh, thanks, Mom. I was wondering why she didn't answer her house phone." He'd been calling her? "I feel better. I thought she believed all the bad things the media is dishing out and didn't want to talk to me."

"Kyle, do you have any idea what Ruby was dropping off in Parker? Or to whom?"

He shook his head, blew me a goodbye kiss and hung up the phone.

We left on that note. We walked out of the building and across the parking area to Larry's Mercedes. It crossed my mind that perhaps Kyle wouldn't have been so friendly to

Larry had he known he was the very person who set in motion the system that brought him there. I chased the thought away. Larry seemed preoccupied with something and kept quiet while we walked. Somehow I knew he was analyzing his conversation with Kyle. This was a silence where I wasn't included, and I was okay with that.

"Do you mind if we have dinner with Bonnie?" He turned to look at me but kept on walking. I stopped, and he reacted to my hesitation. "We need to talk about Kyle and the Porsche. You've seen your son. He thinks he's about to be set free. It doesn't work that way, and I didn't want to be the one to tell him."

I frowned.

"What was that question about Ruby and Parker? You are not thinking about going looking for Ruby, are you?" When I didn't answer he misunderstood my silence.

"Why the sad face?" He took a step back to where I stood, put his arm around my shoulders and pulled me close to him. He did all this in the middle of the sidewalk. Besides Larry and I, there were only a few people in sight. I felt like a teenager being walked home from school. And I liked it.

"You don't mind, then? We're meeting Bonnie next to her office. There's a little place where she likes to eat so we won't take away from her working hours. Okay?" He looked at me and I nodded yes.

I'm doing this for Kyle, I told myself without much conviction.

The aloof expression lingered on Larry's face even as he drove. He put his hand on my knee, but I could tell his mind was somewhere else. "So Kyle is friends with Audrey Bernard?"

I turned to look at him. What a strange question. First Parker, now Audrey. Was he jealous of Kyle? I doubted Larry's loyalty again. "I'm not sure what you mean by 'friend.' They met the same day he got arrested. He spent most of the afternoon with her and would have spent the rest of the evening if not for Carolyn's phone call."

"Carolyn?" He kept his eyes on the road.

"Kyle's agent. I guess he was to meet her at some affair and got sidetracked with Audrey. But the minute Carolyn called, he grabbed his stuff and took off. That was when you two crossed paths." His hand tightened on my knee.

"Can I assume he doesn't know her very well, then?"

"You mean Audrey? It was love at first sight."

"You don't say..." He turned to look at me and his eyes smiled. His smile excited me, a lot. The same sort of excitement as the first time he touched me. I forced myself not to think about it, but I wanted to make him stop the car and make love to me right there and then. I craved physical contact. No, sexual contact—in the worst way. His hand left my knee and found my cheek. He stroked my face with the back of his hand and I sighed. I knew by the way his hand slowed that he felt the same way. We didn't speak, each fighting our desire our own way.

When he did speak, his voice had a whisper of huskiness. "Does he know about the child?"

"The child? What child?"

"I believe his name is David."

"Yes. He met him when he met Audrey, in the garage. She drags her little brother with her most of the time."

"He's not her brother. He's her son."

I turned in my seat so suddenly the impact of the safety belt against my breasts felt like a knife. Larry's hand slid off my face and stayed there in midair. Audrey had introduced herself as David's sister. Why would she lie? And how would Larry know that she was David's mother and not his sister? Who was Audrey to him?

"Looks like Mr. Devin has been busy catching up with Audrey's family tree when he was up in Parker." I regretted saying it.

He slammed on the brakes and stopped the car in the middle of the bicycle lane. With the engine idling he turned to look at me. "Whatever is eating at you, you may as well say it. I understand the stress you're under. I am trying to have an intelligent conversation to clarify just how deep your son is into this mess, and you keep making snide remarks that aren't justified."

I retreated to my side of the car without looking at him and realized how selfish I had been. I'd focused my actions and thoughts of those past days on my obsession with Larry. I needed to think fast, because I had a gut feeling that he was about to turn the car around, take me home and resume his life without me.

"Did your husband cheat on you?" The question knocked the wind out of me.

"No—no!" I had to stop and breathe. "Why would you ask that?"

"Lella, I'm trying to understand why you're so mistrusting. I can't imagine you being like this with everybody, yet around me you make it sound like I'm scheming behind your back. Why would I do that? If I wanted to be in Parker with Audrey, I would be there. So, what is it?"

Whatever I say will make or break this budding relationship. I stared at my hands folded on my lap, praying for the right answer. I looked at Larry, fully aware of my quivering lips. I bit them. I wasn't going to be the poor little crying darling. I heard my voice, and I knew I could tell the truth. "I think I'm falling in love with you and, believe it or not, I'm terrified. This is my first relationship since Nick died. And while I may have had doubts about Nick's loyalty in the past, the new facts that I'm finding out can affect my son's and my life in a way that scares me. What if Nick was cheating on me? And what if that's one of the reasons for Ruby's behavior? I hate being so clueless about people I care about, and you are one of them. I understand people and relationships don't come with a warranty, but right now, that thought isn't helping much."

He cupped my face in his hands and kissed me with such tenderness I felt the world melt with me. I didn't care that we were sitting in an idling car with pissed-off cyclists pedaling by. He held me against him and said my name like the first time in the darkness of the car. A moment like this was worth a thousand miserable ones...and then some.

✦

J.B.'s Court was a small bar and grill. I followed Larry to a table set for three. Bonnie wasn't there. The man behind the bar waved to us. I had the feeling he was going to bring Larry's usual before we warmed the chairs. The layout of the room reminded me of the Old Dana Point Cafe, where I first met Ruby. Same shade of darkness, same mild smell of old rugs and waxed tabletops. We were the only people there.

The bartender set a martini in front of Larry, then sat down on the third chair. "Bonnie called. She's a little late. What can I get your friend?" He looked at me.

Oh, of course, I was the friend. "Water with lemon would be great, thanks."

He didn't seem in any hurry to get me the water. Instead he looked me over like merchandise. I decided to return the favor. He was over sixty, for sure, stocky, not fat, little hair, but bushy brows—one of life's mysteries in my mind.

"How is Olivia?" he asked Larry. Somehow I knew he really wanted to ask about me.

"She's still in Europe. She loves the place. Keeps finding excuses to stay a little longer." Larry's face relaxed when he spoke about his daughter. He fidgeted with his drink, running his finger around the rim of the glass. Was he nervous? Because of me? He shifted in his chair and introduced me.

"J.B., this is my friend Lella. Lella, Joe Basso."

I still tasted his mouth on mine, but I didn't get upset about being introduced as his friend. "J.B. is a retired judge.

Couldn't live away from the courts, so here he is, running a public establishment a block from them." It sounded like a well-worn line.

"Oh, you're the mother of that kid, the movie kid, with the Testarossa."

"Well, it's not his Testarossa, you see." I wanted to tell him to shut up, the way he said "movie kid," just like Bonnie the first day I met her.

Before I had the chance to do more verbal damage, Bonnie showed up. J.B. got off the chair and helped her sit, even kissed her hand. I forced myself to remain an unbiased observer.

Bonnie must be one of those women I'd heard about, but never met. Once they find an outfit they like they order a dozen in all possible colors. Today's version was army green. J.B. disappeared then returned before our greetings were exchanged with a glass of water and a drink similar to Larry's, for Bonnie. Yep, they were regulars all right.

"Did you see Kyle? What do you think?" Bonnie was talking to Larry.

"I know he's an actor." Larry shook his head. "But I can't imagine him putting on an act with his mother."

I nearly spat water over myself. Larry went to visit Kyle to see how he acted with me?

"Yeah, he doesn't have it in him," Bonnie agreed, before I could catch my breath. "The poor kid thinks he's going to be released because they have the Porsche. What did you find out?" How about that? They really met to talk business, and Bonnie relied a lot on Larry for—his opinion? Inside information? What was I doing there?

"Nothing good. Kyle had a thing for the Parker girl, Audrey Bernard. He was over at her place the afternoon of his arrest. Lella said he spent most of the afternoon there." He smiled at me.

"Crap, they'll find his prints all over the place."

I finally spoke up. "Who is going to find his

fingerprints? What are you talking about? What does Audrey have to do with Ruby and the car? You're talking in riddles." Damn, add "inaudible" to my other talents.

They exchanged glances, and J.B. approached with menus. He stood there, not saying a thing. Bonnie looked at him. "I'll have the usual."

"Same here," Larry echoed.

The three of them looked at me, and the owner stuck the menu in my hands.

"I'm not hungry."

Larry shook his head and raised a hand as if to say something. He changed his mind and shook his head again. Bonnie smiled at me like we had some secret entente between us. She pulled the menu toward her. "Lella, J.B. here makes these wonderful sweet potato chips. They're baked and just great with a chicken sandwich he puts together. You should try it. You can always take it home if you can't finish it, but I promise you, it's worth trying."

I shrugged. "Okay." I gave her a ten for effort. Like she said, I could take it home.

"Larry, didn't you tell Lella about the homicide in Parker?"

"What homicide? About the fingerprints..."

Larry put his hand on mine, forcefully. I stopped talking.

"Do you remember the story about Aunt Millie, that Audrey was talking about? Not only was she not her aunt, but apparently, she didn't drown. She was dead before hitting the water."

"Are you talking about the visiting aunt? The one who got along so well with Ruby because they were born the same time and place?" The two of them looked at me like I had sprouted a horn on my forehead.

"You remember all that?" Larry shook his head. "By the way, no, that's also not true. Ruby Russell and Milena Forrester were not the same age, not even close. I think your friend Ruby is five years older. I don't remember the details. They don't matter." I noticed he hardly touched his drink. Neither had Bonnie. "The minute the Bernard girl said her aunt drowned I knew something was up. Parker has what? Four thousand people? You have two women drowning in the same waters the same week in a town of four thousand and it makes national news. I called my buddy, Steve, and he confirmed it. Only one woman, and it was not a drowning nor suicide like first believed."

"Now I remember. You're talking about the drowning victim back when you went fishing? Didn't you say she left a goodbye note or something?" I began to understand. "You're saying that was Audrey's aunt? How come it took so long for Audrey to find out?" Larry and Bonnie exchanged glances again. It was like a curtain falling, separating them from me.

"It may feel like a long time, Lella, but it's only been two weeks. The autopsy was done in Tucson, and then the body was returned to Parker." He stopped and looked directly at Bonnie. "Damn! If she died in California and the body got dumped in Arizona, it means the FBI is going to step in. We're screwed. You'll never get the kid's bond lowered." He drank his martini straight down—the whole drink.

"Want a refill?" I hadn't seen J.B. approach. He bent and whispered something in Bonnie's ear. She too gulped her martini, closed her eyes for a minute. I think I held my breath because I felt a sense of doom in the air.

"The neighbor has identified the woman seen leaving the parking garage at about the time the Porsche magically appeared." There was neither joy nor relief in Bonnie's voice. We looked at her. J.B. stood next to her, his hand resting on the back of her chair, a whisper from her shoulder.

"Was it Ruby?" I dreaded the answer.

"No," Bonnie addressed Larry. "It was Carolyn, the agent."

NINTEEN

The quiet of the room awoke me. The quiet and the dream. The room I could understand. With my own bedroom being so close to the intersection of the 5 and Pacific Coast Highway, I had become attuned to the constant humming of engines. Here, in Larry's home, high on a hill and surrounded by massive trees, all was stillness, darkness. I didn't want to move, afraid to wake him. His body spooned against mine, his arm draped over my belly, his breathing calm and steady while my mind spun endless versions of the dream. When is a dream a nightmare? In the years since Nick's death I had never dreamt of him, not that I could remember. Why now? Why here?

It had to be connected to Larry's question early in the day. "Was your husband cheating on you?" Why the hesitation in my answer? I should have said no, period. I'd been ignoring the ugliness of that reality for years, why stop now?

The digital clock sat on Larry's nightstand. I would have to look over his shoulders to see the time. If I guessed by the darkness it was the middle of the night. When we left Bonnie, Larry drove us to his house. He didn't ask me. It was like a covert understanding. He drove with his hand firmly planted on my knee, his eyes on the road, no conversation. I felt an intense sense of anticipation, a sexual craving that fueled our silence. We went from the garage to the bedroom, shedding our clothes and my inhibitions, ending up on the bed, naked and raw.

I didn't know how long I'd been awake. No matter. I didn't want to close my eyes, afraid to see that image again. There was nothing sinister in the dream sequence. It was Nick's face against a blue background. His image filled the imaginary screen, and all he did was laugh. Laugh. I didn't see myself or anyone else, yet I sensed I was the audience. The more Nick laughed, the more frightened I became. He pointed a finger at me, at the invisible me in the audience, and it felt like the finger reached out from the screen to touch me. I woke up.

Perspiration trickled from my throat to my belly. Long-forgotten details of Nick and Ruby—late-night office meetings and out-of-town conferences—flashed in my mind. I'd learned not to think about it. I wasn't going to revisit that place of sadness.

Nick was dead. Nothing could change that reality. I caught the droplets of sweat with my fingers before they reached Larry's arm. He moved and his hand covered mine, like a shield. I closed my eyes and drifted back to sleep.

⁂

I awoke to the flirting of Larry's lips on my earlobe. "Wake up, sweetie, it's a beautiful morning." He called me sweetie? I smiled before opening my eyes.

I rolled over to face him. He wore a white terry robe. His hair, still damp from the shower, fell to cover part of his forehead. I recognized that clean aftershave smell I had come to link to him. "Good morning," I mumbled, thinking I wanted to brush my teeth before getting too close, but not ready to hop out of bed nude in the light of day. I remembered the time before. "Where did you shower?"

Larry looked at me like I came from some alien planet; then I watched his expression change. "Very observant, aren't we?" He sounded amused and attempted to turn my question into a joke. I wasn't going to let him get away with it.

"Well?"

"When you were here before I showered in the guest bath, wanting you to have a perfectly clean shower. But all that special treatment stuff is over, sweetie, so you can use this shower. Or it would be your turn to use the guest bath." He smiled with his voice and his eyes. "I made coffee. Let me go get you some. Wait, don't say it. I know how you take your coffee." I watched him get up from the bed and fought the urge to grab him, pull him back, hug him tight.

"Oh, almost forgot." He stepped into the bathroom, came out holding a white robe similar to his and threw it at me. "Here, sorry. I couldn't find slippers with rhinestone initials on such short notice." Now his eyes and his face openly laughed. I flung the pillow at him and missed.

"Bad aim." He started walking away. "Hold the thought. I'll teach you when I get back." I could hear him laugh on his way to the kitchen.

What a perfect way to start the day, if I wasn't fighting a sense of guilt in the pit of my stomach. Would be perfect if not for Kyle. The poor kid couldn't seem to catch a break. I started to sound like Larry and Bonnie, lawyers and cops. Okay, enough. I grabbed the robe and went to turn on the shower, changed my mind and brushed my teeth first.

I was stepping out, wrapped in the bath sheet, when Larry rushed in. "You've got to see this. Hurry. Be quiet or we'll spook it."

I didn't have a clue what he meant. He dripped enthusiasm on my wetness. Before I could say a word, he grabbed me around the waist and carried me, towel and all, into the bedroom, in front of the large, round window. He placed a finger on my lips. "Shhh..." Then pointed to a small, adorable Bambi, a baby deer, munching on a tree's lower branches. I had heard of deer living in some of the canyons surrounding Laguna, but in all the years of living in Orange County, this was the first time I ever saw one. A living Disney vignette. We kept still, watching this gift of nature, until a black bird landed on the tree. Bambi leapt back and hopped away. The sight of such a joyful creature had me think of Flash and her empty food dish. I sighed and Larry let go of me and of my towel. I stood frozen, my back against his chest. I felt his fingers caressing my hips, his hands gliding slowly upward to cup my breasts. He stroked the hardness of my nipples. By the time his tongue found my throat, I became a shameless, lustful beggar.

⚬᪣᪣⚬

It was after eleven by the time we got dressed and ate breakfast in his white kitchen. I knew I had to get going, get back home, maybe take a little detour to say hi to Kyle on my way south. Of course, I depended on Larry's goodwill. He was my ride.

I was about to ask when his cell rang.

"Hi, Bonnie." He looked at me. He listened to whatever Bonnie was saying and nodded a few times. It seemed to me whatever was being said must have been good, because he'd nod and look at me with a smile in his eyes. "I will. I'll let her know as soon as we hang up. Thanks, Bonnie."

I knew they were talking about me. I couldn't believe Bonnie didn't know I was right there, next to him.

"Well?"

"How well do you know Carolyn, the agent?"

I looked at Larry. Carolyn?

"I don't know what you mean by 'know' her. I met her once at a cocktail party Kyle took me to. I spoke to her occasionally when she called the house looking for Kyle. Why?"

"Apparently Carolyn has a drinking problem and lost her driving privileges due to some DUIs. That's the good news."

Again I had to look at him, not sure where this was headed. "What's the bad news?"

"To the point, aren't we? Carolyn had nothing to do with the Porsche being left in Kyle's parking spot. She arrived there by cab, went to the condo and got in with her own key, picked up the papers she needed and left in the same taxi. All that in under twenty minutes. That's great."

"Why is it great, and what's the bad news? Or is it good news? How is this affecting Kyle?" Impatience had me shaking.

"With Carolyn out of the picture, Ruby is becoming a more likely suspect. She had the car, she's familiar with Kyle's place—all that according to Kyle, of course."

"Of course."

"How do you think Ruby could drive there, leave the car, disappear and no one sees her? How is that possible?" He asked me. I felt like I had been accepted in the Bonnie-Larry team.

"Maybe she had a friend waiting for her. Maybe she paid someone to drop the car there." None of this made much sense, but I had to keep on talking, hoping I would remember some details or some names. Anything.

"Don't make yourself crazy over this. Every cop in California knows what your friend Ruby looks like. If she is alive, it's—"

I pushed the stool away from the counter, "What do you mean if? She's alive, I know it." The chart of a dead woman. I remembered Nick's laugh and his pointing finger. A cold shiver ran along my spine, like a gust of icy wind. I fidgeted, avoiding Larry's glance.

"What just happened here? Did you remember something? A place, a person Ruby may go to for help? Lella, look at me."

"I need to get home." I didn't look at him. He didn't answer. We sat, waiting each other out. After a long silence, he got up.

"Fine. Let's go." His voice felt as distant and unforgiving as his eyes.

TWENTY

We reached the 5 South without exchanging a word.

What was wrong with me? One minute I soaked in happiness, the next I drowned in anxiety. No, more like I was being drowned. This had nothing to do with Larry; it was all my doing. I couldn't handle emotions, and at the moment emotions ruled every aspect of my life. Better learn how to deal with it. In a hurry.

I talked out loud to myself. "What a week of accomplishments! My son's in jail, more or less accused of killing my best friend, I got fired from my volunteer position at the mission and I managed to anger my lover three times in less than twenty-four hours. Whoa! A record performance, although I can't take full credit for my son's arrest." My brain switched gear too late to stop me. The whole mea culpa came out of my mouth in a very civilized way, almost joyful. I kept my eyes on Larry, hoping for a smile, a change of expression, anything that would give me an opening. At one point, he looked like he sucked in his chest, held his breath. Maybe he fought the urge to talk to me? No, that was it, end of show. Maybe not. Larry sucked in his chest because he was fighting—laughter?

"Are you laughing at me?"

"No. I'm laughing with you."

"But I'm not laughing."

"You crazy Italian..." He kept on laughing. I wanted to hug him, but I wasn't going to push my luck just yet. "It's bad enough I have to take second place to your son. But I'm not going to be pushed around by a cat."

I had to think a moment to understand what he was saying. I told him I needed to get home to feed Flash. I tapped my fingers on his knee and probably would have done it again, but he grabbed my hand and held it in his. He squeezed it gently, then opened my fist and kissed the center of my palm. I knew our relationship had reached more solid ground.

His cell phone went off. I guess he recognized the number because he mumbled some apology, let go of my hand and answered the phone. "Hey, Steve, what's up?" He sounded happy and friendly, yet his face looked tense. "Yeah, well, comes with experience. No kidding. You get what? An average of two homicides per year? Glad I could help. What's going on with the Bernard girl? She did? Interesting."

I assumed Larry was talking to his fishing buddy from Parker. The one who was also a detective?

As soon as he hung up I voiced my curiosity. "Were you talking about Audrey?" I could have asked a dozen of other pertinent questions, like, "Were you speaking to your friend Steve?" But no, I had to bring up Audrey first.

He took my hand, set it on his knee and kept it there. His eyes focused somewhere, past the road to Dana Point, past the distant horizon. "Aunt Millie was dying." His voice came softly, part storytelling and part sad human being. "Brain tumor, few months left to live. She came to town to say her goodbyes. Who would want to kill her? It was a matter of time."

"I'm so sorry." I meant it. I felt sorry for Larry because he felt sorry for Aunt Millie. "How did she die? I mean, how was she, you know..."

He turned his head to look at me, then went back to his driving. "Blunt force trauma to the head." His voice still sounded far away. "She lost her hair during chemo. At first the coroner assumed her wig fell off when she jumped into the water and hit her head on a rock. Once her body got to Tucson, and to the Pima Medical Examiner, it became clear the trauma occurred at least twenty-four hours before she landed in the river. They never did find the wig."

"Is that important? The wig, I mean."

Again he turned to look at me, briefly. I could tell his brain was on overdrive.

"Hair was found in the Testarossa and the Porsche. The hair wasn't human, but synthetic. The missing wig may be the link."

"Why would someone go through all that trouble to steal a—oh my God! That's not what you mean. You think the dead aunt was in both cars? How? What would Kyle want with Audrey's aunt? Wait, Kyle didn't even meet Audrey until the day he was arrested. The aunt was dead before you and I went to dinner at Cannons." I felt my throat closing on me. I knew it was an illusion, but a powerful one. None of this made any sense and yet everything seemed to follow a twisted logical pattern.

"Welcome to the world of homicide investigations. By the way, real aunt or not, Audrey is the only heir, and according to Steve she'll be up in Parker for a while trying to take care of things."

We were approaching the Ortega exit, where the wire fence is painted sea-foam color and metal silhouettes of swallows in flight remind tourists and locals alike that this is the way to the beloved Mission San Juan Capistrano.

"They're getting ready for the parade of the return of the swallows. Wonder what time they decided to ring the bell tomorrow."

"Wait, when you said you got fired from a volunteer job were you serious?" I could tell by his voice he found the idea amusing.

"I've been helping with fundraising for the mission for over nine years, but tomorrow I won't be there."

"Why? What did you do? Besides, what's the big deal? Any organization would be happy to have you."

"I didn't do a thing. The head of volunteers is concerned my presence could be disruptive because of Kyle and the whole nonsense story of Ruby. Makes me sad even if

I agree it's better this way. You know what I mean. I'd rather go visit Kyle."

He patted my hand. "I think I understand how you feel. I spent many Saint Joseph's days running around the mission when I was a kid. Lots of fun, especially looking up in the sky and pointing to the imaginary swallows."

We both laughed, thinking about the crowds traveling for miles to see the return of the migratory birds. So many years since anyone spotted a live swallow around the mission. Word on the street said that they nested at the Mission Viejo Mall because accessibility to water and soil was no longer available in the manicured gardens of the mission. The birds needed those two elements of nature to build their mud nests. But I didn't know for sure if the swallows nested at the mall.

"So, what would happen if you showed up anyway? They'll call security and get you thrown out?"

"I don't know. I never thought about it."

"Maybe you should go and see what happens? I could go with you, borrow a badge to flash around?" The mental picture of me showing up at the mission with a police escort made us both laugh again.

We were still laughing when we drove through the gate to my house. I felt welcomed even if only my cat was waiting for me. A lot can be said for familiarity and habits.

I unlocked the front door and went straight to the laundry room, calling Flash.

"So, where is my competition?" Larry followed me.

I stopped. I sensed Larry's body heat close behind me. The travertine floor of the laundry room was littered with dry cat food.

"Looks like your cat decided to feed itself."

Flash was nowhere in sight. I walked over to the cabinet where I kept the dry food; found the bag exactly where I left it the day before, but now it was empty. There would be no way for a cat to do that, even if it was a genius, which I never imagined Flash to be. I reached for the bag.

"Wait, don't touch it." Larry grabbed me and pulled me away from the cabinet. "Let's talk and let's find your cat." He was trying to play it off, but he sounded like a cop.

"Flash, Mommy is home. Come here." It felt awkward using baby talk in front of Larry in order to coax my cat out of hiding. "She may be hiding under my bed. She does that when something bothers her." A rehash of when I came home from Italy.

I headed for the stairs when Flash appeared at the very top. "There's my kitty. Come to Mommy. Tell me why you're scared." I met Flash halfway, sat on the step and stroked her back, wanting to make sure she was fine. I noticed Larry by my front door. He had the door open and was looking at the lock, shaking his head. "No sign of forced entry. How's the cat?"

I had a feeling Larry wasn't a cat lover, but a caring human being. "Can you store the spilled cat food in a grocery bag? I would like to take this empty one to Tom and have him check it for fingerprints if you don't mind, and then I'll come back and change your locks." He didn't wait for me to start complaining and argue, he kissed me on the cheek and left, but not before I promised to lock my doors and stay put until he came back.

I sat on the couch, Flash still in my arms, but fighting to get away. Kyle was the only one who had a key to my place and he was in jail. Ruby had one, but she gave it back. Or did she? I got up and walked over to my small desk in the kitchen and grabbed the basket where I kept all my keys, but then I remembered I never discarded her letter. The keys must be still in the envelope. Where did I put it? I lifted the stack of discount coupons I saved but always forgot to use and got lucky. I recognized the blue edges of the envelope underneath it all. My hands trembled when I unfolded the crumpled paper with the entwined RR logo. Much had happened since I first opened her mail. I walked over to the front door, inserted the key and turned the lock. It worked perfectly. So much for that thought. "If the keys could talk." I'm not sure why I said that out loud; something about the whole thing just didn't feel right.

I remembered that evening when I unsealed the envelope and the keys fell on the table. I remember thinking they shone like gold. My own keys were silver colored. Oh my God! A new sense of excitement sent tingled up my spine. Was that the way cops felt when they investigated a lead? Nonsense, what was happening here? I walked to the table, the very same table where I'd opened the letter the first time. I could hardly control the thrilling effect brought on by my discovery.

I sat, rested both house keys next to each other. There was no denying the blatant reality; the key sent by Ruby was gold colored and shiny, without a single scratch or tarnish caused by wear, while my own key looked more like a dirty nickel, dull and worn. The key Ruby mailed back wasn't the one I'd given her, it was a brand new copy. She kept the original.

Even little old me could figure out the purpose; she wanted access to my house. But why? What could I possibly have that she didn't? I lived alone on fixed income, Ruby had more money, a better house, more expensive jewelry and clothes, a luxury car, so what was it? It couldn't be Flash, she could have kidnapped my cat while I was gone. Kidnapped? I had to stop watching those cop-show reruns—honestly. If Ruby was here and fed Flash, how did she know I wasn't home? My car was parked in the common garage; I rode in Larry's car. I thought back at my dinner with Larry, the Porsche was parked next to my car that evening when I came back—mio dio—she was in the house while I was here, getting ready for bed. Now the shivers up my spine were pure fear, not excitement. Where could she have been hiding while I went around calling Kyle's name? I bet she had a good laugh at my stupidity. Maybe she was in the house right now. Stop it. I had problems breathing, thinking, standing still.

Hurry, Larry, hurry.

The pantry was the first door I opened; from there I went around clockwise and checked every room, every closet, behind every curtain, even looked under the beds, but nothing seemed out of place, and no trace of Ruby. By the time Larry called to announce he was at my front door I was exhausted.

"You okay?" Larry lifted my face and spoke to me eye to eye.

"Not really, we need to talk." That didn't come out as I intended, well, too bad. I dragged him to the table; after he sat I rested the keys sent by Ruby next my house and mailbox keys. "Well?" I asked, my hands on my hips.

Larry looked at me. "Well what?"

"The keys. Don't you see? The ones Ruby returned aren't the same I had given her."

He pushed back his chair and seemed to study the keys, and me. "You told me you hadn't seen Ruby since before you left on your trip."

I didn't like the way this conversation was heading. "I didn't see her. She mailed back both the door and mailbox keys."

"Did she say why she was returning the keys?" His voice had changed. This was the super-sized charming version he used to gain people's trust. Same caring tone he used with Audrey. He wasn't fooling me. I felt his eyes on me and it made me nervous. "You're sure these are your keys?" Larry held them in his open hand and kept starring.

"They are not, that's what I'm trying to tell you. The front door key is a copy, the one I'd given her was silver colored and the mailbox key doesn't even look similar, it is a totally different key."

Larry looked at me and his eyes had that dark shade of gray, the shade of a stormy sky reflected on the stormy ocean, the same eyes that stole my heart the first time we met. "Let's take a walk to your mailbox."

For the first time since getting home, I was really thankful for his presence.

"Okay, let's."

We walked the path that crossed the guest parking then wound uphill to the cluster of mailboxes. Behind us the setting sun put an orange blush on the tall walls of the villas. "This one." I pointed to my mailbox. I watched Larry attempt to insert the key. He tried in different ways, but nothing worked. Then he tried the key on other mailboxes. That made me feel uncomfortable, but hey, he was the cop.

The key didn't fit anything there. He looked at me with more intensity than usual, and I had nothing to say. I felt validated and a little smug. We headed back to my place without much talking. Larry put his arm around my shoulders and adjusted his pace. I had to get something straight. "So Ruby has the key to my mailbox. No big deal, right? What? She steals my credit-card account? She doesn't need it because she's loaded."

"What kind of person is Ruby?" His arm was still on my shoulder. "What does she like to do? What kind of places does she like to go to? You should know."

"Ruby has three passions: men, wine and jazz. Not necessarily in that order."

"Sounds like the perfect date." His voice was low.

"What did you say?" I pulled away from him.

He chuckled, a soft laugh. "Just making sure I have your attention. Lella, I'm not concerned about the missing mailbox key. I'm concerned about what this key opens. I bet you are right. Ruby kept your original keys and mailed back copies. Somehow she sent back the wrong key, this one." He held the small key between his fingers. "And now she wants it back. I think she came to your house looking for it. Does she know where you keep your keys?"

I nodded. I realized his theory made sense, but had no

idea what this key could open. It reminded me of the keys you use for luggage, or a gym lock.

"Lella, I think you should pack some necessities and come home with me. I don't think it's a good idea for you to stay here alone. If you can't be without Flash, bring the cat and we'll find a comfortable place to put her."

He was willing to put up with my cat? A picture of his spotless white house flashed in my mind, and I realized this man cared for me. Offering to take the cat was worth more than a diamond ring.

"What happened to changing the locks?"

"I intend to do that right now, but I would feel better if you went back with me, at least until we can get this sorted out."

I watched him change the lock on my front door with the ease of a professional. He handed me the new keys. "While you get ready I'll call Tom and Florian and see how they want to handle this new twist, okay?" He kissed my forehead then pulled out his phone. I went upstairs to pack up what I'd need.

TWENTY-ONE

I still couldn't get myself to hate Ruby. There had to be some explanation for her behavior, for the pain she was causing and for the dead bodies dogging her footsteps. I told Larry about Flash, the special gift from Ruby. What happened to that Ruby? Who changed? Ruby or me? Maybe neither. Maybe for the first time I did see the real Ruby. Hiding in plain sight, where did I hear that before? How appropriate.

Larry went to the station to talk to the detectives in charge of the case. I convinced him to go without me. He wanted me to wait in his house instead, but I didn't feel like hanging around an empty house that wasn't mine. The police station was closer to his house than mine, much closer. I told him it would be foolish for him to drive back to Dana Point afterward. I craved solitude, I said, and promised I would keep the phone with me at all times. He had me memorize his cell number, then left with the duplicate keys of the house and the mystery key. The new lock and the fact I had already checked out every possible hiding place in the house helped my state of mind despite Larry's doomsday warnings. I had a somewhat pleasant evening, a nice phone conversation with Kyle and, as soon as I finished cleaning up the mess in the laundry room, I planned to go up to my room and dig out my swallows outfit. I liked Larry's suggestion. Come morning, I would make an impromptu appearance at the mission. As a visitor. I felt like a rebel. Yes. Couldn't wait to see the expression on Sabrina's face. I'll show her.

Flash raced up the stairs ahead of me, back to her playful self.

I reached the last step. The phone rang. Larry.

"Hi, sweetie, how is everything?"

"Fine. I'm up in my bedroom. I checked all doors, and I'll keep the phone next to me. "

"Bonnie is going back to court on Monday to convince the judge to let Kyle out on bail. We need to get it done before someone realizes that Aunt Millie died in California, and then her body got dumped in the river in Arizona. Hey, do you know I've never seen your bedroom, nor your bed? I need to hurry back and visit you."

"Exactly where are you?"

"Exactly?"

"That's what I said."

He sighed. "Parked in my garage. My house is a lot closer to the office than yours is, and after I went to see the guys—"

I laughed. "Good night, Larry. I'll be fine." I didn't want to hang up. By the stepping noises in the background I could tell he was walking up the stairs from the garage to the house. I liked the feel of the phone against my ear and knowing he was doing the same at the other end.

"I don't know if I can sleep without you next to me." What I felt in his voice gave me goose bumps down the back all the way to my ankles.

"I miss you too." It was my turn to sigh, and I really meant it. We hung up.

Except for the hat, I kept my swallows outfit with the winter clothes. I loved that hat. We found it at Tippecanoe's, years ago, when Ruby and I used to roam Laguna Beach in search of unusual things, from antiques to junks.

Before the car accident. Before her marriage to Tom.

Tippecanoe's rated high on our list of fun places. We discovered weird and wonderful stuff. That particular day, I bought the black gaucho hat. She picked a red Italian raffia beach hat. We hopped down the steps leading from the vintage store to the Pacific Coast Highway, Ruby humming "Stairway to Heaven," me wearing the felt wool hat that smelled of mothballs.

It was summer time and to the far west horizon, the sky and the ocean met in a communion of blues.

I got misty over the memories. Oh, Ruby, what happened to you?

I kept the hat pinned on a Styrofoam wig stand, in a huge box on the top shelf of the linen closet to make sure the brim didn't flatten or flip up. The linen closet had the only shelf wide and deep enough for the oversized box. I needed the step stool to get the box down. Thank God, the box weighed hardly anything. My foot slipped from the plastic stool and the box flew from my hands, barely missing Flash and landing upside down on the floor.

"Sorry, Flash." The tip of her tail rounded the corner out of the room.

I picked up the box and found it empty except for the two pins. It was like a bad dream. Who would take my hat? Ruby? Nonsense. I'd had the hat for years. It wasn't the kind of hat worn on the street, especially with the red grosgrain band I added since using it at the mission. One doesn't break into someone's home to steal an old hat.

I knew I hadn't lent it to anyone. Better go check on the rest of the outfit, see if whoever took the hat also grabbed my suede skirt and vest. Why take the stand too? As a matter of fact, why not take the whole freaking box? I stomped back to my room and into the closet. There it was, at the very back, in a dry-cleaner plastic bag, my skirt, the fringed vest and the red silk blouse. I set my Italian boots next to it. Perfect. The missing hat put a wrinkle on my sense of security. I went downstairs and rechecked all the doors and windows while holding the phone. Larry's paranoia must be highly contagious.

⁂

I woke up in a good mood, went through my daily routines with an extra zip in my step and by 9:00 a.m. I hit the road to San Juan Capistrano and the local celebrations. I planned on spending only an hour or two at the mission, and then I could go visit Kyle. He would probably get a kick seeing me in my swallows outfit.

It felt strange going to the celebration as a tourist. A nuisance too. I had to park at the temporary public parking and walk half a mile in my fancy boots with spiky heels while fighting the crowd of locals and visitors. The locals were easily spotted. Most of them wore gaudy Spanish costumes, highly touted by our Chamber of Commerce along with the one-fountain-per-public-building rule. Although laughable in my opinion, all that received high grades from tourist bureaus around the country.

When I worked the phones for the arrival of the swallows, I sat most of the time. As a walking visitor, my feet were on fire, and I missed my hat. My volunteer ID card hung from a thin silk cord around my neck. It guaranteed me free entrance to the mission any time I wanted, but I decided to purchase a ticket out of a sense of fairness. I planned to sneak up on Sabrina and watch her expression. I wasn't mad at her anymore; in fact, I intended to apologize for my rudeness during our last phone conversation.

I didn't recognize the woman selling tickets. How could they have only one person on such a busy day? Her nametag said Valerie. She noticed my ID tag.

"Oh, you're Lella York? Your friend was asking about you. You just missed her." She slid her eyeglasses low on her nose to look at me.

"Sabrina?"

"No, no, Sabrina is over at the gift shop. We were a little short-handed." Her tone was low, as if she were sharing secrets with an old friend. "She didn't say her name. A blonde, dark glasses, about this tall." She put her hand a few inches above her head. She was sitting down, so it meant nothing.

"Thanks, Valerie. I'll go over and say hi to Sabrina." What a relief, she didn't ask about Kyle.

The mission gardens appeared spectacular and luscious

as usual, and a lot less chaotic than the town's streets. People this side of the walls looked as colorful as the ones outside. I walked over to the gift shop. Not sure why this place tended to feel a few degrees cooler than the rest of the buildings. Here visitors spoke in softer voices, and the room smelled of citrus and potpourri. The potpourri was one of our projects. We collected rose petals, orange peels and an array of other fragrant things and tied them in cute little sachets.

I spotted Sabrina by the native jewelry display. She wore her usual white gown with lace sleeves and a red cummerbund. The outfit was originally an old white cotton nightgown and came from Goodwill. But Sabrina performed one of her creative tricks; she added a red cummerbund, pinned a red silk hibiscus in her hair and proclaimed her dress to be a copy of Bizet's Carmen. Two younger docents rushed to the same Goodwill store hoping to score a similar treasure but couldn't find anything even close to it.

"Excuse me, ma'am." I tried to disguise my voice. "Seen any dazzling bullfighters lately?"

She turned to look. Her professional smile died and she stared at me, eyes wide open, mouth even wider.

"Shhh," I whispered. "I'm traveling incognito." I watched her relax. She poked my shoulder with her index finger and we laughed.

"Where is your hat?"

I shook my head. "Gone. I wanted to stop by to apologize to you."

"Forget it." She waved her hand. "Want to stay and work? We're very short-handed."

"Can't." I pointed to my feet.

"Huh! Nice boots. Got them in Italy?"

I nodded. "They're killing me. I bet I have blisters already. I'm sorry." Just the mention of blisters made the pain go up a notch. "I'm planning on sneaking out through the back and driving home—provided I can make it to my car."

"How is everything?" Sabrina was being very diplomatic.

"Good, lots of things happening. We need to do lunch or something and catch up. Okay?" Shifting my body weight from one foot to the other didn't help. I had to get out of the torture devices. "Sabrina, Valerie, the admission person, said someone came looking for me. Any idea who it was?"

"A dazzling bullfighter?" she chided.

"She said a blonde. I've got to find a place to sit before I leave a trail of blood." Whoever said that if you want to forget your troubles you need to wear tight shoes must have owned Italian boots.

I left. I wanted to stop a few minutes in Serra Chapel. Maybe sitting quietly and elevating my feet would help me make it to the car. This was not the way I had envisioned my day at the mission. By now, the morning mass would be over, and with the exception of the very pious, no one would be in the chapel. I could sneak in, rest and be gone. I went halfway up the aisle and sat in one of the pews.

Hard to believe these wooden pews were over one hundred years old. I always felt like part of living history in this chapel, the oldest building in California still used for mass. Even at high noon, the small recessed windows high up by the ceiling let in a filtered light. The scant sunlight and the thickness of the original walls kept the place naturally cool. I remembered the times Ruby would meet me after my volunteer work, and we would stroll down to Sarducci's for lunch. The restaurant, named after the fictitious character from Saturday Night Live, served creative Italian food prepared by a Polish chef.

Right now, though, I appreciated the silence of the chapel most. I sat and put my sore feet on the kneeling bench—what a relief. Incense and the smell of votive candles filled the air while the oil burning inside red glass containers reflected on the gold leafed retablo behind the altar. All that gold had me thinking of the keys Larry took with him, and something else, what he asked me on the way back to the house: "What kind of person is Ruby? What does she like to do? What kind of places does she like to go to? You should know." He was right.

I should know.

And I should be exploring each and every possibility. What was I doing here, moaning about my feet while my son sat in a jail because of my so-called best friend? I needed to get home, change into comfortable clothing and go find that heartless bitch.

What would be the fastest route from the mission to my car? I should avoid Camino Capistrano. The only way to accomplish that meant getting out through the cemetery on the east side of the chapel, and I had a strong feeling that gate would be locked on Las Gondrinas' Day. May as well go out the same way I came in. I braced myself for the lunch crowd, much more aggressive than the morning strollers I bumped into on my way in. Everyone would be cranky, hungry and ready for chips and salsa.

Leon Rene's song "When the Swallows Come Back to Capistrano" played from several speakers, as it did every year. People sat under colorful umbrellas and century-old trees, while waitresses in smocked Mexican peasant dresses hurried around with pitchers of water and margaritas. My prediction proved right. The minute I reached the corner of the mission's wall, I got sucked into the crowd. I was a woman on a mission. What side of Camino Capistrano looked less mobbed? The left side had more shops, so people tended to slow down to look in windows. The right side housed more eateries. Decisions, decisions. I began to cross to the right side of the road when I noticed my hat!

Dio mio, was I hallucinating? Nope, I would have recognized the red ribbon even at a red-ribbon convention. It was my hat. I couldn't see the person wearing it. It moved along with the crowd. Because of the height of the wearer, the hat appeared to be bobbing—now you see me, now you don't.

Damn, I was going to take care of that thief, boots or no boots.

I picked up the pace, pushing my way through people, garnering dirty looks and insults. Maybe it was an illusion, but it seemed as if the hat also moved faster. For a moment I got a better glance and saw it was a woman dressed in black. I could only see her upper back and head. A blond woman. Could I attract her attention? How? Screaming wouldn't help. The streets had enough noise to drown a foghorn.

I got lucky. The blonde moved away from the river of humanity and walked into the covered Capistrano Plaza, past the row of small shops, down the narrow stairs, turning right at the last step and taking off through the parking lot. These parking spots were mostly reserved for customers of surrounding restaurants. She knew the neighborhood.

"Excuse me," I yelled after her, feeling stares on me from people waiting at the train station. I kept moving, painfully aware I could only walk at a certain pace and swearing at my decision to wear the spiky heels. We were tracking back where I came from. "Hey, hat lady."

The woman turned to look at me for an instant. I caught a glimpse of blond hair, large dark glasses and red lips. Those red lips—Ruby!

Oh my God, oh my God. I had problems coping, thinking and moving. I could hardly breathe. I kept on walking, searching my purse for my cell phone. Come on, come on, damn phone. I called Larry's cell. I had a good view of Ruby's back, in a black pantsuit, running at full speed away from the train depot.

Larry picked up. "Hi, sweetie."

"It's her. She's here. She's here," I panted. "What should I do?"

"Lella, what's wrong? Slow down. Where are you?"

"At the mission. It's Ruby."

"Lella," Larry said. "Tell me where you are, and I'll get someone there right now. Stay away from Ruby. You sound breathless. Are you listening?"

"She stole my hat." The silence that followed my statement spoke a thousand words.

"Sweetie"—the snake-charming voice rang in my ears—"are you okay? Maybe you should find a place to rest, and I'll send someone to get you?"

"Shut up, Larry. I'm trying to catch Ruby. Remember her? All the cops in California are looking for her? Well, she is right here, by the tracks, a block north of the mission, and I'm going to get her. You hear me?" No answer. He hung up after I told him my location. He was as familiar with the place as Ruby and I. Damn you, Larry.

I can do this.

She gained ground ahead of me. I knew where she was headed: a small opening in the chain-link fence siding the train tracks to the east. She found it and crossed over, heading toward Los Rios Historic District. Not good. Where were the cops when you needed them? Should I call 911? I pulled out the phone, still trying to catch up with Ruby. It slipped out of my hand and fell to the hard ground. I saw the battery fly one way, the rest of the phone the other.

Why?

Forget the phone. My feet felt fat and heavy, and hard to lift. I had to get over the tracks. The heel of my left boot got stuck in the steel groove, and I couldn't budge it. I looked to see where Ruby was headed but the bougainvillea bushes and the purple vines dotting the low fence hid the road below, and she disappeared out of sight. I was close enough to the train depot to see people looking at me and motioning. I squatted down and began to unzip my boot. It was then I felt the tracks rumbling. The Amtrak Pacific Surfliner was coming in.

TWENTY-TWO

I had a captive audience at the depot. In spite of the tracks shaking and rumbling I unzipped the boot; my foot was so swollen I couldn't get it out. I heard the people waiting for the train calling to me. How fast could the train be going when it needed to come to a complete stop fifty yards from here? No time to find out. I wiggled and twisted and pulled. Come on. In a desperate attempt to free myself from the tracks, I stood, took a deep breath and then jerked my foot back hard. It came loose, but something snapped and I lost my balance, falling on my behind. I heard folks clapping, laughing.

I wasn't going to leave my boot there to get run over, I could always sell the pair at the consignment store. One person's torture devices could be another person's footwear from heaven. I retrieved my boot a split second before the steel mammoth roared by me. The gush of air from the row of passenger cars zooming by lifted my skirt. I jumped back, one boot on, one off. I heard the hiss of the train coming to a stop at the nearby station. The thing must have had great brakes.

Someone grabbed my arms from behind and pulled me farther from the train tracks. "What are you doing?" an angry woman's voice said. I wiggled myself free and turned to look at this tall, thin woman with short hair and a stern look on her face. She wore a frothy chiffon dress, open sandals and some silver jewelry that rattled like my cutlery drawer every time she moved her hands.

We stared at each other. "Mrs. York, just what were you thinking?"

"You know me?" When I said that, her expression relaxed, she attempted a smile, and little wrinkles formed just above the bridge of her nose. "Flor—Detective Florian?" I didn't have a clue as how to address her. "You look—different."

"It's my day off." She sighed. "Devin called." She looked me over. "What were you doing?" Her impatience barely concealed.

"Why did he call you?"

"He called everybody. I live in Laguna Niguel, so I happen to be the closest to you." She pronounced "you" as if it left a bad taste in her mouth.

I had a strong hunch she wanted to call me something else.

"I was trying to catch Ruby."

She looked around. "Where is she?"

Was she mocking me? "She went that way." I pointed to the west side of the train tracks. "Los Rios. I'm not sure where she's headed. And then my heel got stuck in the tracks." I could tell she didn't give a hoot about what I was saying. She wanted to get back to her lunch. "Shouldn't you be calling for more cops to come and comb the area?"

Florian looked at me for a long time. Was she ignoring my question? I fidgeted with the left boot still in my hand.

Finally she spoke. "Can you walk?"

I put my foot on the ground and pain shot all the way up to my knee. I wished to die, but I wasn't about to let that snotty young lady know, so I smiled. "Of course I can walk. My feet are just a little sore. I was running in heels trying to catch up with Ruby."

"I'll get the car and drive you home." She ignored my reference to chasing Ruby.

"I have my own transportation, and I can drive myself home. Thank you. However, if you would be so kind as to help me get to my car...I'm not sure I can get the boot back on." I held her stare. I could tell she was weighing the pros and cons of her next move.

"Where's your car?"

"The other side of El Camino Real, around the corner, in the public parking by the Egan House. I was heading that way when I spotted Ruby. She's a blonde now." Judging by her expression, the more details I shared, the less she bought my story. I shut up and took painful little steps. While I hung onto her stiff arm, we walked in the direction of the parking lot.

"If you don't believe me, ask all these people." I pointed to the train depot. We turned our heads to see the empty platform and the train slowly pulling out of the station, heading south to San Diego.

Her deep impatience hung over me. I had ruined her day off. I was realistic enough to know I needed help, so I stopped and got the car keys from my purse. "Florian, would you mind bringing my car around? It's all I need, honestly." I handed her the keys. Conflict shadowed her face. Frustration won.

She grabbed the keys "What's your license plate?"

"Huh?"

"Your car, the license plate of your car?" We looked at each other and her judgmental eyes reminded me of that American eagle you see on anything patriotic, from stamps to national parks ads. Damn.

"I—I don't know it. Wait. It's a Ford Mustang, silver-gray, with a custom dark gray stripe on the hood."

Florian checked me over deliberately from my bare feet to my gray roots. The look on her face declared she hated me. What could I say? If I was her, I'd probably think I had it coming.

She left, walking quickly toward the parking lot. I tried to retrace my steps. Maybe I could find my phone. I hopped around, careful where I put my bare foot, diligently picking harmless spots to land on. I got lucky. I found the battery first then, not too far away, the rest of the phone. I wanted to try to reassemble it, but I heard a car horn—my car horn. I looked up and saw Florian, standing by my car. What a wonderful sight. I dropped the battery and phone into my purse and hopped toward her.

She didn't move, made no attempt to come and get me. The short distance felt like the trek to the Promised Land. I reached the car. Florian handed me the keys without a word.

"Thanks, Florian. Thank you so much."

"You're welcome." She turned around and went up the short alley.

I sat in my car. My butt hurt. I bet I had bruises. Too bad, I had to get home. Most importantly, I had to get out of here, in case Florian kept an eye on me. I switched on the engine and headed out of San Juan Capistrano. As soon as I got out of Florian's sight, I parked on the side of the road and removed the other boot. The minute I took it off I felt instant relief—wonderful. With both feet freed of the harnesses from hell, I could drive home. Or not.

I felt a noticeable difference. The right foot started to be normal but sharp pains shot from the toes of my left foot all the way to my brain. Oh, oh. I lifted the foot up on the seat and massaged it. The closer my fingers inched to my big toe, the more the pain intensified. Could the foot be broken? Maybe the toe? I couldn't put any pressure on it. It looked huge and getting bigger by the second. No way to wear shoes with that toe. I started the engine again, made a U-turn and headed for the emergency room at San Clemente Hospital.

Chasing Ruby would have to wait.

I gave a watered-down version of the facts to the admitting nurse then sat in the quiet lobby and waited for a doctor to look at my foot. I had time to analyze my encounter with hat thief. Was it really Ruby? My Ruby? I went back through time, to see if somewhere along the way I missed important clues. Never mind that. All I saw was a blonde wearing my gaucho hat. In all the time I'd known her, Ruby never wore such enormous dark glasses. The only familiar aspect was the luscious ruby-red mouth. Then again, this wasn't about appearances.

Mind games popped into my brain. What would Ruby gain by playing cat and mouse with me? Maybe it wasn't about me at all. Maybe it was about Ruby and Kyle? The more I analyzed the events in my mind, the less sense they made. Ruby had a lot more money than Kyle or I. Except for the lingering side effect of the accident, she was in good health. With Tom dead, she turned into a healthy, wealthy, good-looking single woman. For all practical purposes, she appeared to be invisible too. Two days before I left for Italy we had lunch together down at the marina. I forced myself to revisit details of the lunch to see if she acted differently than normal. We ordered the same food we always did. Soup and salad for me. Chicken and coleslaw for Ruby. And a glass of wine. We both had wine. I drove away, leaving Ruby at the marina because she needed to run some errands, and I, of course, had to get home and start packing. The next time we saw each other, she picked me up to drive me to the airport. If changes had taken place in Ruby's life, she hid them well. Either that or the Ruby I thought I knew never existed. Was she created by the real Ruby to gain my acceptance and forgiveness? Nah, who was delusional now? Every time I felt the need to give Ruby absolution, memories of Nick at the funeral home found their way into my consciousness. That and my son Kyle, in a cell for something he didn't do. Would an unbiased outsider assume that Ruby's ultimate goal was to destroy my family? Oh, dear God. I never thought about it that way. I felt like someone punched me in the middle of my chest.

"Ma'am, are you okay?" The voice of the woman behind the desk brought me back to reality.

I smiled at her. Nodded. "Yes, thanks. I'm fine."

My doubts and my fancy rationalizations began to fade once again. Drama, my life seemed to have become a series of dramatic events. All in need of closure.

What about Larry? He called Florian. I managed to ruin Florian's day off. She didn't believe a word I said. Did she tell Larry about rescuing me? Did it matter? I knew my name would be mentioned among Larry's co-workers. I decide not to dwell on it. I needed to focus on finding Ruby. One thing I knew for sure—for the first time since Ruby's disappearance, I feared my old friend.

TWENTY-THREE

My toe was sprained, but not broken. Thank God for that. The doctor taped it to the one beside it, then he bandaged my whole foot and told me that only time and staying off my toe would help. He suggested taking an over-the-counter painkiller if necessary. The cute nurse gave me a pair of non-slip socks, the kind surgery patients wear. I hobbled back to my car and headed home, feeling physically better but emotionally drained. I drove into the common garage. Larry's Mercedes sat next to my parking spot. The driver's door was wide open and his legs hung out. Uh oh. I expected him to jump to his feet to greet me or perhaps yell at me. He didn't do either. I parked next to him, grabbed my evil boots, locked the car and gingerly walked toward the Mercedes.

"Hi." I smiled.

He stared at me. I sensed his irritation; what did Florian say to him? "Are we back to not answering the phone?" It came out as a sigh. He was concerned about my wellbeing, I assumed.

I rummaged into my purse, looking for the broken cell phone. Larry must have noticed my no-slip socks for the first time. "What happened to your shoes?"

What? Detective Florian forgot to give him a detailed report? Besides, my boots were in plain sight, dangling from my hands. Not sure what element nudged his consciousness, but something did because he got to his feet. "Sweetie, are you okay? You're limping. What happened?"

If he tries to carry me, I'll slug him, I swear.

"It's nothing. I broke my toe."

"How did you break it?"

"Let's not waste our time discussing my feet." Did I

really say that? I must have. Larry looked at me with a whole different attitude, or at least that was how I credited the smile overtaking his usually brooding eyes.

"Need help?"

I relented. It hurt walking on that hard concrete.

"Yes, please."

He kicked his car door shut, walked over and hugged me like you hug something or someone very special and dear. I got so choked up I nearly dropped the boots on my good foot.

He put his arm around my waist. "Lean on me, take the weight off the foot."

We walked over to my place like an old couple, in perfect harmony.

"Did you talk to Florian?" Like it or not, I needed to discuss my chase with someone, to test my sanity. He was the perfect someone, a trained detective with an invested interest, I hoped.

"I thanked her for lending you a helping hand." He didn't look at me.

"Do you believe me? It was Ruby I saw, I swear. Were you able to find out something about the small key she had mailed me?"

"Okay, one question at the time. Regarding Ruby, other facts support the possibility of the woman being alive and roaming around." He shook his head. "It's hard to believe she hasn't been caught. She must have some means of transportation, and a place to stay. She isn't invisible. The theory that she changed her appearance is also a possibility. Regarding the key, I'm told it's a safety deposit box key."

I sat on the couch next to Larry. "You said a safety deposit box? Like the ones people get at banks for important stuff?"

"Yes, that kind of safety deposit box. Can I get you something to eat or drink?"

"Larry, I'm fine. Do you need anything?" I didn't give

him time to answer. I had noticed Flash's absence. "Where's my cat?" As if on cue, Flash appeared at the laundry-room door and walked over to sniff my new socks. "Come here, my little baby," I called to Flash. "Come sit with Mommy."

Flash jumped on the couch and rubbed against me, purring. She sniffed the boots. "Those are the evil boots that gave Mommy a booboo, and now Mommy can't wear her shoes to go see Kyle. Poor little Kyle."

Larry watched the whole scene without a word.

The truth hit me. How was I going to visit my son if I couldn't wear shoes? Would I be allowed in with open-toed footwear? I couldn't remember the jail dress code regarding shoes. Damn! Flash jumped off the couch and went straight up the stairs to my bedroom. So much for socializing.

"Lella, do you have any other outside doors beside the entry door?"

"The patio door, but no key there, it slides. Are you still concerned about Ruby and my old key?"

He smiled at me. "Comes with the job." That half-devil-half-angel smile lingered on his lips and gave me pleasant goose bumps. "Have you considered installing a security system?"

"Not really. I've always felt safe here."

"You don't even have a peephole on the door."

"Can we talk about something else? Like, Ruby, Kyle, the safety deposit box..."

"Let me look at you. Is that the costume you wore at the mission? You went there after all, didn't you? That's my girl." Larry sat next to me and I remembered the phone. I pulled out the parts and the battery and handed them to him.

"These are the pieces of your cell phone?"

I nodded. "Can it be fixed?"

"That's why you weren't answering." He pulled me closer and began to reassemble the phone with his arm around my waist.

"I dropped it while chasing Ruby. If not for the boots and the train, I could have caught her or the blonde who stole my hat. I think Ruby is both people. That doesn't sound right, but you know what I mean."

"Tell me about the hat."

"You don't believe me, do you? Neither did Florian, I could tell. I can show you pictures. I wear the hat every year for Swallow's Day. It's sort of my signature. But the box was empty this time. My hat was gone, along with the wig stand I kept it on."

I felt the arm around my waist tense. Something I said must have hit a nerve.

"You kept your hat on a wig stand?"

"Upstairs, in a huge box. The box was in the linen closet. But when I got it, only the pins were left."

"I think you're onto something." He said it in a hushed voice, talking to himself? "And you think Ruby wore a blond wig?"

"No, I never mentioned a wig. I said she was a blonde."

He handed me the phone.

"Oh, thanks. Is it working?"

"Looks like it. How close did you get to this hat thief?"

I couldn't tell if he was trying to get information or just making conversation.

"She outran me from the very beginning, that's because of my poor feet. I only saw her face for a few seconds, from a distance. But those red lips, ah, that's so Ruby."

"Lella, why would she steal your hat, then come parading it around the mission?"

"I don't know, I've been asking myself the same thing. Maybe she wanted to make sure I was there working." I had not thought of that before. "We were together when I bought the hat. She's done crazier stuff than taking a hat since her accident. What am I saying? Ruby likes to take chances. Maybe she needs the adrenaline rush. It got worse the last year or so. It's like she forgets and she goes backward."

"Backward?"

"Yeah, one time she withdrew a lot of money from her own account. And she made a big production of telling me Tom, her husband, didn't know about the account. Then insisted she had no recollection of it and had no idea where she stashed the money. Or when she went looking for me at my old house, months after I had moved out. The doctor assured her it would get better, that it was a matter of time. I don't know. I'm tired of talking about Ruby. I need to find a way to get to see Kyle."

He sat next to me, quiet, his arm still around my waist. The arm was still there, but the mood not so much. Larry's body was there, his mind wasn't.

"Can I get you something? Water, coffee, soda, wine?"

He moved a little away from me. "No, thanks. I'm fine. Yes, I know it's your house and all. But I'm here, at your service." His voice came from a faraway place. He looked through me, not at me. "Sweetie, do you mind if I make a couple of phone calls?" He already held his cell in his hand.

"Sure, go ahead." I started to get up. My foot felt pretty good, all things considered. "I'll go upstairs and change my clothes while you do that."

He didn't answer. I could hear him hitting the numbers on his mobile. I began climbing the stairs. It had to be something I said, I knew it. I remembered how I felt when I discovered that Ruby substituted the keys. My sense of elation. Larry exhibited the same symptoms.

Flash, sprawled on the bed, watching with an expression of pure cat boredom while I removed my skirt and examined the damage. Nothing ripped, but even so, the hard landing left noticeable marks. I would try to clean it with a hard brush. I had undressed down to my red silk camisole and my undies when I noticed the flickering on the answering machine. There was a message. "Hello, Mrs. York, it's Audrey, your neighbor. I know I—asked you to keep an eye on my place while I'm in Parker, and I just wanted to say, well, don't be alarmed if you see people, I mean, movers. Things have changed since I arrived, and I need to stay here in Parker indefinitely. I would appreciate if you could say hello to Kyle for me. Maybe you could keep me posted if anything new comes up and thank you for all your help. Goodbye." What?

Before my brain could process Audrey's monologue, the house phone rang. Kyle?

"Hi, Lella, It's—" Bonnie? Calling on a Sunday evening? Oh my God. Something must have happened to Kyle.

"Is Kyle okay?" I blurted out before she could finish her sentence.

"Kyle is fine. I just left him. We had to work on the details for tomorrow. We'll be in court in the morning. I suggest you get there no later than 9:30 a.m.. Actually, I insist you be there. We need to show he has family and friends' support, ties to the community, people who care. Carolyn, his agent, promised to come."

"I'll be there. I'll be there, even if I have to come barefooted. What's happening? The cops found Ruby?"

"Barefoot? I don't understand." No comment regarding Ruby.

"Nothing, a stupid joke. Tell me about Kyle." I heard Larry coming up the stairs.

"There is a good chance Kyle will be able to go home. Even without locating Ruby. He will be monitored and confined between home and work. We got lucky. He was cleared of the arson charge—"

"The what? Arson? My son was accused of setting fire— to what?"

"Calm down, Lella, that part is over. With new evidence of Mrs. Russell being alive and bent on mischief, we don't even have to post bond."

Calm down, Lella? She spoke of my son's jail and life as if it were a routine business. What was wrong with her?

"Anyway, got to run. I'll see you tomorrow, and maybe

we'll get a chance to do lunch with Kyle and Carolyn before Kyle gets shipped to his condo." What was she saying? His condo? Why? "Good night. Say hello to Larry." She hung up.

I was dumbfounded. What did Carolyn have to do with Kyle's release? Was there a reason Kyle couldn't stay with me? If he was going to be house bound he would need someone to take care of him. How did Bonnie know Larry was here? I felt like I was being stared at. I turned around, and there was Larry, standing by the bedroom door, looking at me.

"That was Bonnie," I informed him.

He walked over and slid his finger under the shoulder strap of my cami. I didn't expect that at all and instead of responding, I froze. Larry kept his finger there and tilted his head to meet my eyes. I don't know what he read because I felt so overpowered by contrasting emotions. He was getting a taste of my feelings in thirty-one flavors. He let go of me when his cell chimed.

"Hi, Steve, thanks for calling back so fast. Yes, that's right. So it was a blond wig Milena Forrester wore. It's just a suspicion. I think you should talk to Bob. Yup, he got my desk after I left." I sensed a sort of sadness in Larry's voice. Did he miss his job? "Yes, you're right, with Florian. Let me get you his cell number. What's there to lose? Just curious, did Forrester have a driver's license? You see where I'm going with this. My cell, it's best. Yup, you got that straight." He hung up and now his eyes had a new glow, a newly found passion, and unfortunately, I didn't think it had anything to do with my red cami.

TWENTY-FOUR

I watched him breathe. In the shy light of dawn, Larry's face looked relaxed and passion free. What a captivating impostor he would make, I knew. I practiced with him the excesses of desire. He was the first man ever to lie in this bed of mine, this custom-built with a view of the ocean. The view was the last thing on my mind. I had to get to court before 9:30 a.m., and Monday morning traffic would be a killer. Should I get ready before waking him? Or endure more of his funny questions about my magnifying makeup mirror and my multiple jars of age-defying potions and lotions? I got out of bed and went to make coffee. I owed him that for all the perks I enjoyed at his place.

One thing I learned from our hours of twilight bonding, he really did miss his job and considered going back. He also explained about Kyle and the arson charge. Mrs. Snoopy had called to report that Kyle's Porsche was parked at the Russells' house the night of the fire. By then Kyle didn't have the car. Ruby had already made the switch. I didn't say much but was willing to bet that Ruby set fire to the house. At this point I didn't even believe the story of her brain injury. No, she was plain evil from birth and good at manipulating people.

I fed Flash, put the coffee on and went to shower in the guest bathroom. When I got back to my bedroom with two mugs of coffee, I found Larry sitting up, enjoying the reflections from the shimmering ocean and scratching Flash's belly. Oh my God, what a sight! Add all that to Kyle's release, and this could possibly be one of the best days of my single life.

By 8:30 a.m. we locked my door with the new key and headed for the garage. We crossed paths with a man carrying a wooden post and a sign. It was a real estate sign, FOR LEASE. I grabbed Larry's arm, forcing him to slow his pace. I wanted to see where the sign would be posted. The man stopped in front of Audrey's place. I remembered her message. Movers would be showing up, and she wasn't coming back. My day went off the charts.

I wore open-toed sandals with low heels. My pants covered most of the footwear, so unless I stood up and limped, no one would notice my problem. The swelling had gone down, and I felt okay. We approached the ramp to the 5 North, chatting about Bonnie and Kyle. The traffic was light, but we knew it wouldn't last; once we hit Irvine the lanes would get crowded and slow. At least we wouldn't have to change freeways.

I looked at Larry. "Are you coming to court, or are you waiting outside?"

"It depends. I'm hoping to hear from Bob. I had my friend Steve call him about Aunt Millie and your old friend the hat snatcher."

I smacked his knee, and he laughed.

"What about it?" I asked.

"I have this theory. What if Ruby is going around pretending to be Milena Forrester, a.k.a. Aunt Millie?"

"Why? They look alike?"

"I doubt it, but picture this, same wig, dark glasses—who knows? She may be using Aunt Millie's ID to get around incognito."

"The ID of a dead person?"

"Lella, you know she's dead because I told you. I know because Steve told me. But the world outside of Parker doesn't know about Aunt Millie or Milena Forrester, and unless someone digs deeper, it's possible her death isn't even showing up in some police databases yet." He looked at me, and I shook my head. "Shake your head all you want, I think it's brilliant. I suggested they get the media to run with the story, showing the photos of both women. How about that?"

I nodded. "The way Ruby looked when I chased her, if not for the hat I wouldn't have given her a second glance. You may be right. I can't wait to see Kyle. I'm so excited. Do you think he'll be wearing his own clothes?"

"Women. How can you think about what he'll be wearing? And frankly, what does it matter?"

I was happy. He could tease me all he wanted. "I'm not sure I'll recognize Carolyn. It's been a long time."

"I'm sure she'll recognize you." He put his finger under my chin. "Who can forget this face?"

"Keep your eyes on the road and your hands on the wheel." Still smiling at his compliment.

We were approaching the loop where the 405 and the 5 split, where it was typical to see a car with a confused driver zigzagging in and out of lanes like the tail of a kite in a hurricane. Today, the confused driver of a tan SUV swerved into our lane. Larry yanked the steering wheel to the right, without braking. We missed the SUV by inches and ended up in the emergency lane. The Ford truck behind us wasn't so lucky. It T-boned the SUV, sending it fishtailing against a two-door white car in the next lane. Metal to metal and crashing glass. All cars came to a stop in a squealing of brakes and an acrid cloud of smoke. It was over in minutes, yet from my passenger seat it felt like forever. Thank God our airbags didn't deploy. They did in the truck. I could see the airbags, but not the driver or any passenger.

Larry checked on me. "You okay?"

I nodded, shaky and searching for my voice.

"You're sure?" He sounded cool and in control, already dialing for help.

"Yes," I managed to whisper.

"Stay here. Don't leave the car. You may get hit by some onlooker. I'll go see if I can help."

I had no intention of leaving the car. At the moment of the near accident, I anchored my feet against the floor with all my strength, more as instinct than wise decision.

My left foot was killing me thanks to the open-toed sandals and the pressure I put on the toe. More vehicles pulled into the emergency lane. Curious witnesses began to pour onto the freeway. I looked at my watch. People may be injured, even dying, and I was concerned about getting to court on time, yet I couldn't feel bad about my train of thought. Kyle's wellbeing meant everything to me.

The Ford truck seemed to gather most of the attention. The first to respond was a motorcycle CHP. He parked his bike behind the Mercedes and didn't seem to notice me sitting inside. I watched him reach to his holster then talk into his phone. Checking in? He walked toward the truck, where the small crowd assembled. Larry stepped away to meet the highway patrolman. They spoke a few words and then went back to the Ford. Why all that commotion around the truck? Soon the rest of the emergency vehicles announced their arrival in an impromptu parade of lights and sounds.

It was 9:20 a.m., and I assumed Kyle was seated in court by now. Did I bring my mobile phone? Yes, thank God. There wasn't much for me to do from my premium seating except wait for Larry to come back with an update. The "telecopter" from KTLA5 circled the sky, more red robin than buzzard with that racy paint job and flashy lettering. The traffic was now getting channeled into the car-pool lane and, of course, every vehicle slowed down to ogle. I watched Larry shake hands with a paramedic—looked like the two of them knew each other— then Larry walked back to the car.

"I am so sorry." He sat in the driver's seat and rolled down the window. "I know how important it is for you to be there with Kyle. Unfortunately we need to stay put until one of the officers takes the report and the whole scene has been mapped out. It may take hours."

"It's okay. It couldn't be avoided." It wasn't okay. I fought the urge to scream my frustration for everyone to hear.

"If I knew which judge they are seeing I could get a message to Bonnie, but I don't know, and there are no phones in court."

"Really, Larry. It's okay," I lied. "By the way, why is everybody gathering around the truck? What's going on?"

He shook his head. "It's a very young couple. The woman is eight months pregnant. She's just a kid herself. A little thing, like you." He smiled at me, stroked my knee. "The airbag hit her hard, and she may be going into early labor. She's being shipped to the hospital, and the paramedics are treating the old man in the white car." We watched the ambulance lights go on, and the vehicle began to move. "We were lucky, and so was the son of a bitch who caused all this mess. It never fails that the culprit walks away unscathed." I saw the motorcycle cop coming in our direction.

"Here we go." Larry got out of the car.

<hr>

The sun shone high in the sky by the time we started to move. My watch said 11:30 a.m. Kyle's fate was probably sealed, and I had no idea what happened, nor did I know why Larry looked so broody.

"Larry, is something bothering you?"

"As a matter of fact, yes. It's that Ruby. Slippery bitch, isn't she? I'm beginning to take this personally. She's playing games with you and therefore with me. I will find her."

"Can I help? I'm twice as fed up as you are. I thought she'd be hiding at Kyle's place, but instead she just dumped the Porsche there. Maybe the three of us can sit and explore possible hiding places."

"The three of us?"

"Yes, Kyle, you..."

His cell phone went off . "Oh, hi. Really?" He turned to look at me. "Don't know. Let me ask her. Lella, do you have your cell?" I nodded. "Bonnie says your son has been trying to get in touch with you, but you're not answering."

I searched my handbag and pulled out the phone. I pushed button after button, but it showed no sign of life. "I forgot to charge it." I sighed.

Larry held his cell by his ear. "Her phone isn't working. Wait, I'll put her on. She can talk to him." He handed me the phone.

I heard some background noises, cars going by, then Kyle's voice. "Mom?"

"Kyle, oh my God! How are you? Are you free? I'm so sorry I wasn't there, oh, Kyle—"

"It's okay, Mom, I heard about the accident. It's okay. I'm out. Carolyn is here. I'm going to have to wear one of those ankle monitors—Mom, where are you? Will I see you before we go?"

"Where are you going? We are on our way there."

"We're at this place called J.B.'s Court? A friend of Bonnie's owns the place. We grabbed something to eat while waiting for the car."

"What car?"

"Oh, Carolyn leased a car. I'll have to drive because she still has a few months to go on that DUI before she gets her license back. Anyway, we'll be leaving once the car gets here."

"Kyle, I need to see you. I know where that place is. We're on our way. Tell Carolyn she must wait, do you understand? I'm going to hang up because I'm using someone else's phone. Please, wait." Tears rolled down my cheeks, and I felt uncomfortable. The last thing I needed to do was get overemotional. I handed the phone back to Larry. I wanted to ask him if he heard about J.B.'s, but I wasn't sure I wouldn't end up sobbing. I kept my eyes focused straight ahead and my lips tight. Larry put his hand over mine, and we drove absorbed in a silence bursting with emotions.

TWENTY-FIVE

I rehearsed what I would say to Kyle. To make sure I didn't break down and cry, practicing was the best way. We arrived at J.B.'s grill. I recognized Bonnie's dark green Land Rover. Parked out on the street, bound to get noticed, was a beige sedan. Kyle stood by it, talking to an androgynous-looking individual. Carolyn! I had forgotten about her bony frame and angular features. With her hair cropped inches from the scalp, her lack of makeup and her dark pantsuit, she could easily pass for a man. Except for the outrageous, elaborate earrings she wore all the time. Today it was gold sea shells with black beads. Maybe it was intentional, to stand out in a male-dominated world? It seemed to work, judging by her success. Kyle wore a suit I had never seen on him before—Carolyn's idea? I remembered Kyle telling me she had a poster in her office stating, "Image is Everything."

Larry made a U-turn and parked next to the sedan. I couldn't wait. I jumped out of the Mercedes and landed on my left foot. Ouch! I didn't want my toe to become the subject of the conversation.

"Mom!" Kyle ran to hug me, looking surprised. I realized he didn't know I drove up with Larry.

I heard Carolyn in the background, "So, are you the cop?"

"Kyle, let me see you. You look great. How do you feel? Is it all over now? You don't have to go back there, do you?" Kyle was the same age as Nick when we first met. He looked so much like his dad. Why was I thinking about Nick?

"Mom, slow down. Too many questions. We can talk about that later. I want to tell you about the Italian reporter."

"What Italian reporter?"

"RAI TV, the Italian broadcasting system. They had a reporter in court, Pia Bartolomei. Cute girl." He had the same dreamy look on his face he had when he met Audrey. "All the way from New York. She's working on a special about first-generation Italians in America. That, plus Carolyn has a script for me, from an Italian director." Kyle spoke so fast and with so much enthusiasm, I had trouble taking it all in. "Mom, I'll need to practice Italian. I may go to Italy. Won't that be fun? I can visit my cousins and the home you were born in."

"Whoa, from jail to Cinecitta?" I was lost on how this fit in with the case.

"Is he telling you about the proposal we received from Italy?" Carolyn asked.

I turned to talk to her and saw Larry going into J.B.'s. He must have sensed my eyes on him—he turned and smiled at the three of us, winked at me and disappeared behind the stained-glass door.

"Okay, boys and girls." Carolyn spoke to no one in particular. "Time to hit the road. You two can chat on the phone. Chop, chop, let's go." She acted like Kyle's fairy godmother, and in a way she was. "Hey, Lella, did the kid show you his new bracelet?"

What was she was talking about?

"Carolyn, come on." Kyle didn't sound too happy. He lifted his right leg, pulled up the pant leg, and I saw this square thing attached to his ankle. It looked like a cell phone case mounted onto a wrist band.

"Oh my God, does it hurt? Is it heavy?"

"No, Mom, it's not heavy. Don't know why Carolyn had to tell you about it." He scowled.

"Big deal. She would have found out either way. Let's go."

Nothing she said could put a damper on my happiness. I hugged Kyle again. He sat in the driver's seat of the Ford Taurus. I stood on the sidewalk, watching the car drive away until I couldn't see it anymore.

Walking into the dim light of J.B.'s place played tricks on my eyesight. I saw dancing shadows where there were none. I tried not to limp. Bonnie motioned me over. Today she wore the brown version of her standard outfit and sat at the same table, on the same chair where she sat the first time, as did Larry and J.B. Maybe our chairs had invisible nametags, because the seat left empty was the same one I had occupied the last time. Larry and Bonnie had their martini drinks and, to my surprise, a glass of water with lemon waited for me.

"Bonnie, I'm so sorry—" I started.

She looked up and stopped me with her hand. "Forget it. Better that way. If you had been in court we'd be still there talking to the annoying Italian reporter."

"Kyle thought she was delightful."

"A week in jail would do that to a youngster," J.B. piped up. It sounded funnier than it was. "We took a vote, and we are all having the same food we had before."

"Fine by me." I swore I felt a collective sigh of relief circle the table. Was I such a royal pain?

"With a little luck, I'll never have to look at this stuff again." Bonnie pointed to a large yellow folder with thick black writing on it.

"What is it?" I was the clueless one, as usual.

"Evidence, copies of everything they have. In case we went to court. Ain't going to happen." Bonnie hummed the last words. "That flighty bitch is about to get caught."

"The police found Ruby?"

"Not yet." Larry shook his head.

I wanted to keep the conversation going. "What kind of evidence?"

Frost shrouded the table.

I looked at their eyes. They looked back. Larry put his hand over mine.

"Okay, what's going on?"

"It's from the safety deposit box. Ruby is still looking for that key. She doesn't know you turned it over to the authorities." That was the longest statement I had heard J.B. make. I noticed his arm was draped over Bonnie's chair. Maybe that was why he sounded so happy.

"It would be a good idea if you spent the night somewhere else," Bonnie advised me. "She's bound to try to get that key."

"Good, I would love to have a chat with her. I don't intend to spend my life in hiding until Ruby gets caught."

"I doubt you'll have to wait. Ruby needs the key now."

"Now? What makes you think that?" I'm not sure why I asked that specific question. The three of them exchanged glances. Bonnie opened the folder and spilled the contents on the table. "This." She pushed a see-through plastic envelope toward me. Everything seemed to be sealed in clear plastic. I picked up the bag and pulled out what looked like a mock passport. United States of America. I glanced at Bonnie.

"Go ahead, open it. It's a copy."

I opened it and Ruby's photo smiled at me. A much younger Ruby. Her last name was still Alexander. How old was this passport? I meant to look at the issue date when her birthdate caught my eyes. "Because of the wrong birthdate?"

"What?" It sounded like a chorus.

"It says December twenty-ninth, 1948. She was born in 1952."

Bonnie rummaged among the plastic-looking documents. "Easy to figure out. Here is her birth certificate. Let's see. Yes, it says 1948." She looked at me as if looking for confirmation.

"She kept her birth certificate in a security box?" I took it from Bonnie. How bizarre. "Why would she lie about her age?"

The three of them laughed.

"Lella, why do women lie about their age?" Bonnie chided. "Why are you taking this so personally? It's only four years."

What was I going to say? Because I spent the last four weeks torturing myself over the chart of a dead woman? Unbelievable! I had no one to blame but myself. I cleared my throat, searching for something to say. "What's so special about the passport?"

"It's about to expire." It was the first time Larry spoke about the security box contents, and his voice sounded— peculiar. Somewhere, in the archives of my mind, a deceit flag went up. I looked at the passport again and Larry was right; it was set to expire on March twenty-fifth, 2006. Saturday. Damn. "You think she needs to get her passport before it expires? Why?" My question waited out there, for anyone and no one in particular to answer.

"To get out of the country. Isn't that obvious?" J.B. said to me.

"I'm missing something. I've known Ruby for a long time. She never spoke of friends or relatives outside the United States. Come to think of it, she never spoke of friends or relatives in the United States, unless you count lovers."

"Bingo," Bonnie said.

We sat quietly for a while, drinks untouched. I couldn't figure out what they knew that I didn't. "How is she going to get out of the country? Swimming?"

J.B. laughed softly. I waited.

"She had tens of thousands of dollars cash, in small bills. Here's the receipt."

"That doesn't get you far." Larry glanced at Bonnie.

Maybe there was a magic password mentally exchanged, permission to wreck my soul. The attitude at the table changed. We huddled around, touching, talking, looking at every piece of copied evidence. Bonnie was familiar with all of this. She explained to me, in no particular hurry, what each item meant, piece by piece.

"She kept some sort of journal. There are time gaps, and the longest one corresponds with the car accident on Ortega." Bonnie may have remembered my husband lost his life in that accident because she paused, shoved papers around and sipped her martini. "See this? I'm not a hundred percent sure, but I bet it's an offshore account, and the money feeding into it doesn't come from a business or investment. It comes from individuals."

"You mean like donations? Secret admirers?"

"Secret admirers." J.B. laughed out loud. "You funny, girl!" He poked my arm lightly.

"Try blackmail." Larry looked at me. "Ever met any of her lovers?"

I shook my head to fight off mental pictures of Nick's smile. Ruby and I were best friends. She spoke freely of her promiscuity and the married status of some of her lovers, but she never mentioned names. And I had never found this unusual, so which of us was the strangest? "Do you have names? Do you know for sure?" I turned to Bonnie.

"Nah, she posted dates, initials and amounts. Although some initials do correspond with names of prominent married citizens in several newspaper articles she kept and from her own fashion reports. Sleek bitch, indeed."

Out of curiosity, I moved the short pile of copied article clips in front of me to look at the dates. Was she doing this after I met her? How could I be so stupid? My table companions watched me finger through the sheets of paper. I felt like a peeping Tom. I pushed the stack away, and one page slid off. I recognized Nick's smile before anything else. The earth stopped spinning, and blood rushed to my head. Ortega Highway Settlement was the headline. Oh my God! The article went on to describe the accident: The car was westbound on Ortega Highway when the Honda CRX skidded and plunged over the embankment. Eighty-seven accidents had been reported on that stretch of Ortega Highway—two were fatal. I wanted to stop reading, needed to stop reading. But I couldn't. The CHP called the accident site, about fourteen miles east of Interstate 5, "Ricochet Alley." Ms. Alexander, the passenger, was slightly injured. Her companion, Nicholas York, lost his life. Ms. Alexander sued Caltrans. The lawsuit was settled out of court. Marko Forrester was the Irvine-based lawyer representing—Ruby Alexander.

My hands shook. The others looked at the papers, then up at my face.

"Lella, you okay?"

I glanced at Larry and nodded. "Can I take all this home with me and look it over? I'll return it promptly, I promised."

"You didn't know about the lawsuit?" Bonnie sounded puzzled. "Did you notice the name of her lawyer?"

"No, no, had no idea. But I would like very much to have a copy of everything if I can't have your copy." Did Kyle know about it? He did say Nick was driving Ruby's car. Her companion. What else was going on under my nose that I didn't know? I reached for the plastic-covered evidence on the table and started to go through it again item by item, but now I was rushing as if my life depended on it. Beads of perspiration clustered on the back of my neck, and my body quivered like my hands. Nothing looked familiar—names, faces, places, Ruby's other life. My anxiety bordered on paranoia.

And there it was, his picture. I stopped, closed my eyes. Breathe, just breathe. Was I mixing reality with dreams? Nick, looking out at me, laughing, finger pointed. The Nick of the dream. Mocking me? The photo was unusually large, the size of computer paper. But he didn't smile for me. He was laughing and pointing at the person who took his photo.

TWENTY-SIX

A few hundred yards away from J.B.'s place, Larry stopped the car. I knew what would come next. Should he take the 5 South or the 55 east?

"I want to go home."

He didn't argue. The stroke of his hand on my knee felt different, more tender than sexual. "Something happened in there. I know it. Care to talk about it?"

I shook my head. I didn't trust myself not to break down.

"I figured it has to do with Ruby and—Nick." He said "Nick" in a hurry, devoid of emotions. Was he going to play cop? He started the car and headed toward the 5. "Aren't you even a little curious about that lawyer, Marko Forrester?" I knew he was changing the subject to get my mind off my worries.

"I assume he's related to Aunt Millie?" His good intentions worked, if only a little.

"He must be. I don't believe in coincidences. None of this will matter as soon as Ruby is apprehended. Bonnie had all that paperwork in case she had to go to court with Kyle."

"I owe a big thanks to you and Bonnie. Kyle looked so good, like jail never happened."

"Could help him if he ever plays a convict," Larry said. Cute.

We entered the freeway. It was still afternoon, yet the lights were lit on the big green directional signs that leapt at us, one by one against the cloudy sky.

"He was in her bedroom."

"The house that burned?" He understood.

"No, that was Tom's house. She met Tom after the crash."

Larry kept his eyes on the road, squeezed my knee lightly.

"They had sex. I could tell by his hair." I had to pause and breathe. "He was getting dressed in front of her bedroom window when she took his photo." I waited for Larry's "so sorry." He surprised me with his silence.

"I have no idea when it happened, and he looked too much at home for that to be a one-time fluke."

"How long did she live in that house?"

We were having this civilized conversation about my cheating husband and my double-timing best-friend slut, and we didn't mention their names, like an unspoken alliance.

"She was already renting the place in Laguna when I met her, and she lived there until she married Tom. It used to be a garage that was part of an estate. A little remodeling changed it into a cute cottage. The entire estate sold two years ago to some French celebrity, a shoe designer or something. Soon the old buildings got torn down to make room for new ones, and I'm guessing they're still fighting with the city or the Coastal Commission, because nothing has been built." We approached the spot of the morning accident, except now we traveled in the opposite direction.

"Wonder if that young lady in the truck gave birth?" I was grateful Larry once again changed the subject.

I didn't ask him to come in; I needed to be alone, to hide my pain from the ones I loved. He left, and the minute I got upstairs I collapsed on my bed, hugging myself in a fetal position waiting for the flow of tears to run its course. The phone rang. Not now. It stopped, then the shrill sound started again. Maybe it was Kyle. "Hello."

"Lella?" Bonnie, and she sounded like the Bonnie down at the marina, the day the cops searched my house.

"Yes?"

"Lella, you left in a state of despair. I know it sounds like nonsense, but we both know I'm right. Talk to me, not as your son's lawyer, as a woman, as a friend if you can. What did you see in the file? What did you learn today that you didn't know before? Open up, it will ease your pain and may give us more insight into Ruby's mind. The way the woman thinks, the way she behaves. The police have experts trained to do just that, study people's lifestyles. Like you said, Ruby didn't have many friends. She had you. Lella, you are the link. It may not occur to you right now because you are distraught. Take your time, think about it. Make notes if necessary, even the slightest detail may be the info we need to help us find her."

Bonnie had a distorted view of what a woman to woman or friend to friend talk should be like, and I had no intention of explaining it to her. I had my own list of things to do regarding Ruby. There was one question she could answer for me: "Bonnie, do you have any idea how long Ruby had been friends with Marko Forrester before—you know—the Ortega car crash?" I couldn't get myself to mention Nick's name.

"I don't know how long Forrester and Ruby had known each other before the accident or the filing of the law suit against Caltrans. I do know there was a lot more going on than client-lawyer relationship. Forrester ended up in a mental institution not long after the lawsuit was settled. Perhaps they locked up the wrong person."

"I'm assuming Forrester is still—locked up?"

"Your assumption is correct. I heard a detective from the Santa Ana Police Department interviewed him, or at least tried to. The mind is gone, forever. Results of a crack-cocaine overdose; the doctors were able to save his body, but not his brain. Anyway, you think you can at least give it a try? About Ruby, I mean? Anything else you'd like to talk about? " Bonnie's voice and attitude had changed as our conversation progressed; it morphed from the marina Bonnie to Bonnie the lawyer faster than a snowman melting under the desert sun. Time to say goodbye.

"I will think about it, I promise. Goodbye Bonnie, and thanks again for all you did for Kyle." I hung up.

I didn't lie when I said I would think about it. Think about it? I had been obsessing about it from the minute I set eyes on that duplicate file. All I wanted to do was to wipe the smile off Nick's face. I couldn't. Next best thing would be to wipe Ruby off the face of the earth.

My husband and my best friend.

Lovers.

Cheaters.

Liars.

They made a mockery of my trust, my loyalty, my love. And one of them was now working hard to destroy my son. She would not succeed. Her dark side existed all along, and as usual I chose the path of less resistance. Look the other way, Lella. Never stop believing. This too shall pass.

No more. Bonnie and Larry were right; I knew Ruby better than anyone else. Time to put my knowledge to good use. I mentally revisited the afternoon events and the conversation I had with Larry on the drive back. We spoke of Ruby's old place. The place with the grand view where Ruby filled her rainy afternoons listening to Miles Davis, sipping wine and apparently having sex with my husband. I remembered the days I spent at her place, helping her to recover from her mental confusion, and I remembered something else, her tendency to "go backward," like the time she went looking for me at the house I had already moved from.

What if...what if she went back to her old address, even if the building was gone, the property was gated, the place deserted, safe and secluded—what if. The thought lit an itch in me, a need to know, to find out—what if.

I undressed in a hurry, grabbed my workout pants and a sweatshirt and hesitated only a second before I put on my jogging shoes. The toe still felt painful, but a sense of urgency possessed me. And a sense of purpose, something I hadn't experienced for so long it felt like I tasted it for the very first time. I knew I had to get there before sundown. I ran out the door without checking on Flash.

Ruby's old place was south of Aliso Beach, on the ocean side of the Pacific Coast Highway. On this late Monday afternoon Laguna wasn't as chaotic as it would be in few months. The place was a hub of colorful confusion, laid-back people crossing here and there, and cars parked in hop-scotching patterns off the side streets. I headed toward South Laguna, with its plethora of quaint restaurants and small art galleries sustained in essence by local patrons. In this older part of Laguna some of the beach cottages dated back to the 1900s. That abundance of mismatched dwellings created a hard-to-miss distinction between Laguna and the rows after rows of pink houses to the east of the freeway. I drove by deserted beach parking. Maybe it had to do with the clouds littering the sky. My Mustang climbed the hill like a steed on a chase, and knowing how close I was to Ruby's old place raised my anxiety level.

Would I be able to find the driveway? It was always hard to see it from the road, and no doubt it was designed that way. I remembered the old rusty gate and then the private street dropping straight down, to where the house stood. The garage was created as a shield between the gate and the house. I hadn't thought about that place in years. Memories of jazz and the smell of brine came rushing at me. Memories of the days I spent helping Ruby to get well. How could I have been so blind? Blind? More like blind, deaf and dumb.

I saw the "No Trespassing" sign.

The gate.

My heart pounded in my throat, and I felt sick.

There was no place to park. Across the street from the gate, hundreds of homes, cottages, duplexes on stilts, covered the steep hill, clumped like flocks of lovebirds, colorful and charming, all without parking spaces. The cars of the residents could be found parked on the east side of Pacific Highway, day or night, in rows and close together like links of a chain. On the ocean side there was no parking allowed, and green containers lined the west curb. Trash pick-up day. That wasn't enough to stop me today. I squeezed my Mustang between the garbage cans, forcing a few to push forward.

I got out of the car and walked up to the rusty iron gate. I stretched my neck but couldn't see anything past the rocky path unwinding under the ancient trees and the bushy, neglected edges. My mind wanted to revisit the image in the photo. I wasn't going to let it.

I shook the gate. It groaned, but didn't budge. I walked back and forth the length of the gate, the width of the frontage, not willing to surrender to a piece of metal. What could I find in my car to help unlock this gate? The only thing in my trunk was a gallon of water, an umbrella and a beach chair. None of these items had been needed or used in years. Dio mio, the beach chair! The excitement of the discovery had my hands trembling while opening the trunk. I unfolded the low canvas chair and propped it against the whining gate. Standing in the center made the chair wobble and try to fold close on me, so I grabbed on to the gate with both hands and pulled myself up. That was when I saw it: the roof of the cottage. I recognized the dark shingles. Farther below, the spot where the house once stood was empty, cleaned out, allowing for a patch of sky and ocean to show through. Oh my God! The old garage turned residence was just the way I remembered it. Had to get down there, had to. Damn gate.

I read somewhere that if you could get your head through an opening, your whole body would fit too. Maybe I could squeeze myself between the metal bars? Would I dare push my head through first? Nah. I slid my foot between the bars, then my leg. No problem. If I was going to do this I may as well do it right. My purse was in the car, my car keys in my pocket. I put my hands on the last bar of the gate, the one closest to the lock. It looked like the one offering the least resistance. I pushed my right shoulder in first, then my right leg. Forget the head; if my butt can slide in so will the rest. While the bulky sweatshirt wasn't helping with the sliding process, it softened the pressure of the rusty metal against my chest. I panicked when my head got stuck. I couldn't move, couldn't even wiggle my nose. God! What now? I was hyperventilating, and sweat trickled down my neck. I should have brought my cell phone with me. I should have told Larry.

Then a miracle happened. Perspiration covered my forehead, my face. I pushed my head one way, then the other way. It hurt and I wasn't sure I was moving anything until I felt the bridge of my nose touching the bar. Just like that, my head was free, and I found myself on the other side of the gate.

I stood, listening for a police siren, a dog barking or some neighbor shouting at me. Nothing.

In spite of the adrenaline rush, the distance from the gate to the cottage felt like pure agony. Only gravel covered the path where Ruby used to grow rose bushes, and the place looked locked and in dire need of a coat of paint. The second-story windows were boarded up. I couldn't see a thing either way, yet something inside me had me believing she was there. I walked around the whole building. At first I couldn't come to terms with the fact that it was standing, untouched, and with the exception of the boarded windows, pretty much the way I remembered it. When I came to see Ruby for the first time after the accident, the roses were dying. I brought them back to life, the roses and Ruby. Double-crossing, back-stabbing Ruby.

I was trespassing. I knew that. If I forced the door open, would I be destroying evidence? I pulled the sleeves of my sweatshirt down to cover my hands like I used to do as a child in Italy when I had forgotten my mittens. First I tried pushing, pulling. Then I banged on the front door with both fists. I held my breath, waiting for something to happen. I figured Ruby didn't want to attract attention, so she would come out of hiding to shush me. I figured wrong. It was getting late, and the sunlight was fading. The big trees were dark silhouettes against a painted sky. A sense of gloom hung in the air. I kept hitting that locked door, over and over, for the weeks of pain and frustration I carried bottled inside. I banged my fists until I no longer could then I squatted on the gravel, my back against the door, and wept.

A grating noise came from up the hill. Rusty hinges being forced open. God, oh, God, the gate. Someone opened the gate. The only way out was through that gate. I held my breath and waited. No birds chirping above. No waves crashing below. Only buzzing of distant engines on the PCH disturbed the evening stillness. I couldn't wait. I stood, wiped the tears off my face and wobbled up the driveway toward the gate.

TWENTY-SEVEN

I saw the shadow first. A dark silhouette standing inside the open gate. I walked to the top of the steep driveway with an attitude, attitude being the only thing that kept me going. Because of the setting sun I had trouble making out the person staring down at me. One thing I was sure of—it wasn't Ruby. The man standing there with crossed arms and looking at me with much disapproval was Larry. My Larry.

How did he know where to find me? Before I could think of something to say, he cleared his throat and kept on staring. No smile, no hello, the silent treatment.

"How did you find me?"

"I didn't come here looking for you."

"Oh! Who did you come looking for?" No, no, I didn't mean that at all.

I heard tires screeching, doors slamming, voices. Soon I recognized Detective Bob, Florian and four more people heading our way.

Larry moved closer. "How did you get through the locked gate? What did you do down there?" There was nothing friendly about his voice or his attitude.

"I squeezed between the bars. Down where? You mean the garage? Nothing, I knocked on the door, but no one answered." Did he hear my uninterrupted pounding from the gate?

He looked at my sweatshirt. I followed his gaze; large rusty spots covered my chest area. "Did you touch anything? Tell me now. Would we find your fingerprints all over the place?" It was more a hiss than a whisper.

"Oh, yeah, fingerprints and DNA. I peed in the bushes." Did I really say that?

The cops reached the gate; if they didn't expect to find

me there they hid it well. Bob high-fived Larry, who had moved away from me, and Florian smiled to me, a real smile, wrinkled nose and all.

"We got the search warrant along with the owner's blessing." Bob headed across the property. "Let's see if there's electricity like they claimed."

The other cops walked down the driveway toward the garage. I didn't know what to do with myself. My instinct was to tag along with the rest of them and see what was inside the building. A long, cold stare from Larry kept me from moving. Did Larry follow me here? I didn't like his attitude.

"Would you like to wait in the car?"

"Wait—for what? Why can't I go down there?"

"It's official police business. They may want to ask you a few questions about your presence here."

Anger bubbled inside me; none of this police business would be taking place had it not been for me. Then I remembered I never told any of them, and especially not Larry, about the location of Ruby's old place. Damn. Was I a suspect? I had to stop watching police shows on TV, honestly.

"Okay, I'll wait in the car." I grabbed my beach chair that Larry had moved away from the gate and walked toward the street, planning to get into the car and drive myself home. If they wanted to ask questions they knew where to find me. Looked like Larry had that all figured out. The Mustang I left sandwiched between the sidewalks and the garbage cans was now blocked on the street side by Larry's Mercedes. I was stuck. The rest of the unmarked police cars were parked pretty much where they wanted, including neighbors' driveways. I didn't turn around to call out to Larry to move his car. I felt his stare on my back, literally. I wasn't sure I could control my anger; how dare he? I unlocked the Mustang and got in. I revved up the engine, another thing I would not do under normal circumstances. I started to move the car back and forth, drive, reverse, inch by inch. Since I only had inches, the movement caused the nearest trash can to slide sideways. Now I had more than a yard. Time ticked away slowly; after I managed to move the second trash can I came to my senses. What was I doing? All I had to do was walk out there, move all the bins back to their homes and drive away. Let smarty pants Larry explain all that to angry neighbors.

The containers were much heavier than expected; one in particular appeared wobbly, and I had trouble keeping it upright. At this point Larry must have realized I meant business.

"Lella, what do you think you're doing? You'll cause an accident."

"I'll cause an accident? You're the one blocking my car."

"Okay, okay, let me move my car."

The first vehicle to hit the brakes because of Larry's Mercedes happened to be a Channel 4 news van. Super! I really, really wanted out of there. Larry started to move his car away from mine; I pushed the gas pedal, barely missing a garbage can, and I headed south without looking back.

By the time I crossed the Golden Lantern intersection, my adrenaline rush had faded, replaced by the slow, simmering pain caused by the truth. I couldn't get myself to stop thinking about Ruby's place without thinking of Nick and Ruby's sweaty nude bodies groping each other on her black mahogany bed. Did he whisper endearing words in her ear while caressing her breasts the way he did to me? Where was I when this was going on? Could he actually touch me and tell me he loved me while the taste of her skin lingered on his lips?

By the time I got home and parked my car, I was limping worse than before. Too much time spent on my feet. The doctor warned me to stay off the sprained toe. I unlocked the front door and turned on all the lights, then sat on the couch, drained. Being alone in the house gave me permission to unleash my sorrow.

Ruby and Nick, why? He could have asked for a divorce, a legal separation. How about her? My best friend. Why Nick? She had all those men. I only had one. Now I sobbed without shame. Tears fell on my sweatshirt, and my chest shook. I couldn't talk to Kyle in this state of mind. I had to calm down. I clicked the remote, and the TV came on. Maybe it would take my mind off my problems. CNN and the news. Ruby's smiling face flashed on the small screen, next to another woman's face.

My phone rang. I picked it up to make the ringing stop. It was Kyle. "Mom, are you watching CNN?"

"Yeah," I said, but nothing could stop him.

"It's Ruby and that Parker lady, remember? Ruby has been using her driver's license." He sounded breathless.

"Let me listen."

"Mom, do you think Ruby did something to the Parker lady? Did they know each other?" I couldn't hear what the anchorwoman was saying. Soon the news switched subjects.

"Kyle, I don't know what to say. You were the last one to talk to Ruby, remember? I have no idea what the relationship was between her and Aunt Millie."

Minutes passed. "Kyle, are you all settled in?"

"It feels so good to be home. I took a long, long shower, a hot shower, and I'm in my skivvies, drinking a beer, talking to my mom and watching TV. Life is good."

"Kyle, did you know anything about Ruby suing Caltrans for the car accident?"

He paused for a long time. "Are you talking about Dad's accident on Ortega?"

"Yes."

"No, never heard a thing about it. When did that happen? I mean, she was pretty screwed up, mentally, you know. You remember her phone calls and all that, don't you?"

"Yes, that's why I was shocked when I found out. It must have been while I was in Italy. You'd think someone from Caltrans would have spoken to us about it." I dried a defiant tear with the back of my hand. "Marko Forrester, a lawyer from Irvine represented her. He may be related to the dead lady from Parker."

"No, never heard that name, but you know what? I'm going to check it all out on the internet."

"You can do that?"

"Of course, Mom. If there was a court case it will be public information. Let me write down the name, Marco Forrester."

"Kyle, Marko is with a K."

"That's an unusual spelling. I'll check it out and call you back."

He hung up before I had a chance to object. The phone rang again. That was fast detective work.

"Don't you have call waiting?" Larry, the real detective.

"No, I think it's rude to make people wait while you decide who gets priority. Anyway, I was talking to Kyle."

"How's he doing?" His voice had that same edge I sensed earlier at Ruby's place.

"He's fine. What happened in Laguna? I'm assuming you didn't find Ruby, or it would be all over the news."

"She wasn't there, but she'd been hiding there. We found trash, a cooler, basic survival stuff." He stopped talking and I held my breath. What was he thinking about?

A good minute went by. "You don't trust me, do you? Is that why you didn't want me to know where Ruby used to live? I have access to records, information, you know? Not a big dark secret. The woman is a criminal; she could hurt you. Don't you understand?"

I kept quiet because I knew he was right. I also knew I would do it all over if I had to.

"Lella, we found the hat."

"Ah! I told you, I told you. It was her." I wasn't talking, I was yelling. I felt vindicated.

"Yes, sweetie, you told us. I apologize for the whole

police department being wrong." Was he mocking me? "The hat is evidence, and even if it wasn't, it's flat, like someone stomped on it."

"She probably did that after I chased her at the train depot."

"We figured that's when she moved out too."

He called me sweetie...so all that silent treatment was because he worried about me?

"We saw the news, CNN. And you were right." That was all I needed to say.

"Ah, ah, Miss Negativity. What did I tell you? Ruby bought a used car in Colton, of all places. She used Aunt Millie's driver license and paid cash. Since the story ran, tips are coming in fast and furious. The salesman who made the sale said she was blond with dark glasses. She bought a generic-looking used white Ford Focus, with temporary plates, unless she switched it with a stolen one." I could hear him breathe. "Sweetie? Are you there?"

"Yes, and you were right. I bet they want you back to work lickety-split, heh, Sherlock?"

He laughed. I wanted a hug.

"Lella, every cop from LA to San Diego is looking for Ruby and that Focus. Promise you aren't going to open your door to anyone, okay? Kyle is under house arrest, and I'm on my way to Santa Ana with Bob. No one should be knocking at your door tonight. No one with good intentions."

"I promise. Do I get my hat back?"

"What? Honestly, you and that hat. It's evidence. I'll take you out tomorrow, and I'll buy you whatever hat you want, okay?"

"Okay. Larry—what did the place look like?"

"Empty and sad. Ruby was camping out, sleeping on an inflatable beach mattress. I doubt she spent much time there. Don't torture yourself." His words told me he understood my pain, my doubts. "There wasn't anything personal."

I sighed. "I'll talk to you tomorrow. I bet Kyle is trying to call me. He's doing his own investigations."

Larry laughed. "Night, sweetie."

I hung up. The TV was still on CNN, but on mute. They were running Ruby's story again. Finally they switched to a commercial, a cat-food commercial. Flash! Damn. I forgot all about my cat. She was probably upstairs under my bed, mad as hell because I was gone all day again. I looked at my toe, the size of a summer squash. Maybe I could bribe her into coming down to eat. "Flash, where are you?" I chanted from the couch. "Where's my sweet little kitty? Come say hi to Mommy, and I'll give you a treat." Silence.

Time to switch to Plan B. I dragged myself to the kitchen, grabbed a can of tuna from the cupboard and started the electric can opener, keeping an eye on the stairs. The can was open; the tuna smell filled my nostrils. No cat. Where could she be hiding? I walked over to the stairs, holding the can of tuna and feeling pretty silly. "Flash, baby, come get your treat." I left the can there and went upstairs, careful not to put pressure on the left foot. I looked and called and cajoled, but Flash was nowhere to be found. Could she have gone out? I had a cat door that she hardly ever used. For some reason she didn't like it.

I went down to the laundry room. I couldn't tell if she used the kitty door or not. It wasn't locked. I kicked it with my good foot. It didn't move. It should have swung open and then closed. I tried again, same results. I got down on my hands and knees and tried to figure out what was keeping it from moving. It swayed back toward the inside of the room. One of my geranium pots was in front of the outside opening. Damn. That idiot yard man did it again. I must have told him a million times to stay off my patio. I liked to take care of my own plants. Squatted by the cat door, I felt pretty stupid myself. I tried calling again, put my face by the opening, "Flash, are you out there, little darling?"

"Meow." The sound was feeble. I wasn't sure if it was

close, wasn't sure if it was my cat's. "Meow." Closer now. It had to be Flash.

"I'm coming, baby, be patient. Mommy needs to get her shoes, and she'll come get you, and then she'll fire the bad man who locked you out." I walked to the couch while talking, got my right shoe on, changed my mind and limped toward the patio door barefooted. I looked outside. There should have been a moon. Instead the clouds had tarnished the night sky, and there wasn't a star or a speck of moonlight.

It reminded me of that night on Ponte Vecchio. New shivers and old fears found their mark.

"Meow, meow." Louder and closer.

I went to open the patio door.

TWENTY-EIGHT

The sliding door had always been hard to open, tonight more than ever. I pushed it enough to stick out my head. "Flash, are you out there?" Nothing. Shoulder against the door, I pushed harder. "Flaaash, Mommy is home." A black fury hissed by, flying past my legs.

I turned to look at her, "Whoa, Flash...where are you coming from?"

"From hell." Ruby's unmistakable voice rose from the darkness. Before I could react, she thrust the weight of her body against mine, forcing me backward. I tripped and landed on the living-room floor. I sat, stunned. We looked at each other; the only sound came from Flash gulping the tuna I'd left on the stairs. Ruby stared down at me, at my awkward position, my bare feet, her smug smirk heightening my sense of nothingness.

"Ruby? What happened to you?" My own voice surprised me—calm with a hint of concern, trumping the rumbling I felt in inside. "You look exhausted." That wasn't what I meant to say, but I didn't dare tell her she looked awful.

"That's because I'm in a hurry. Where's the key?" The blond wig, already askew, slipped a little farther to the left, her bright red lipstick smeared on her cheeks.

"What key?"

She kicked me. I instinctively rolled into a fetal position. Her pointed shoe hit my left toe. I moaned.

"Oh, poor Lella, did I hurt you?" She taunted, then kicked me again.

I grabbed her leg in midair and pulled. She tried to hold on to the étagère next to the wall, but couldn't. She hit the ground with a thud.

We rolled on the floor, fighting for control. Ruby pulled my hair, and I pulled hers. Her wig came off and all went still. I had known all along she wore Aunt Millie's wig, but feeling it in my hands and seeing Ruby's usually curly, shining hair now matted and stuck to her scalp was so disturbing I found myself feeling sorry for her. She must have felt my hesitation. She moved back, away from me, and I began to get up. When I looked at her again she was on her feet with a gun pointed at me.

"You have a gun?"

"You have a gun?" She mimicked my accent.

I still held the wig and didn't know what to say to avoid enraging her. She walked backward to the open patio door, keeping the gun aimed in my direction and, without turning around, she shut and locked the door. "Good, now we can talk without interruptions. Get me my key and my wig, and I'll be on my way."

"This isn't yours. It's Milena Forrester's wig."

For a moment the hunger in her eyes dimmed, only to rekindle more voraciously than before. "What the hell do you know about that fucking loony? Besides, it's my wig, not hers."

"Why do you need a wig? You look so much better without it." I needed to keep talking, keep her calm while I figured out what to do next.

"Haven't you heard? Blondes have more fun." She laughed, and for an instant it was like old times, the two of us chatting, joking. The only missing items were a bottle of her favorite wine and two stem glasses.

"Would you like a glass of Chardonnay?" Anything to get her to put away that gun.

"Are you really that stupid, or do you think I am? Because I'm not, so it must be you."

"What did you do to Aunt Millie?"

She winced. "Would you stop calling her Aunt Millie? You make her sound like a sweet little old lady. Her name is

Milena Forrester. Now get the key so I can get going."

"Why did you kill her?"

She took a step in my direction and lifted the gun. I raised my hands to cover my face. My tremors were so strong I could hear my teeth clatter.

"I didn't kill anybody, you hear me?" Her voice a shriek. "She got sick, threw up all over your bathroom floor. I spent the whole afternoon cleaning up after her, and as a reward, she accused me of ruining her brother's life. A family of fools. Bad genes."

"You mean her brother, Marko? The lawyer?"

Her whole attitude changed. She bit her lips, stared at me, searching for an excuse? "Yeah, that prick." She wiped her mouth, smearing more lipstick. It made her look even more insane, removed from reality. "You give 'em a little head, they think they own your ass. A goddamn coke-head, he was. That's how he fried his brain. I had nothing to do with it. He's right where he belongs." She mumbled the last part and wiped her mouth again. "The key. Now!"

The phone rang.

"Don't touch that phone. I'll blow your fingers off."

"It's Kyle." My voice had the same make-believe calm as before.

"Kyle?" She laughed. "Poor baby, getting lonely in his cell?" She didn't know about his release?

"Yes, he's sitting in jail for something you did. Why? What did he ever do to you?"

"Please, don't start one of your holier-than-thou tirades. As soon as I'm safely out of the country, starting my new life, I'll make sure he goes free."

"How?"

"I've written a letter. It explains how Milena got sick."

"How did she get sick?"

"Stop interrupting." Beads of perspiration dotted her upper lip. Ruby looked nervous. "She tripped on Flash coming down the stairs, hit her head. I told you she started throwing up. I had promised her a ride home. Drove her to Parker. She kept nagging and falling asleep, then she puked in the car. I'd had enough. I locked her in the trunk."

"You what?"

The phone stopped ringing.

Ruby looked at me with those dark, insatiable eyes of hers. I needed to sit, but pangs of fear twisted my brain, and I didn't move.

"Lella, I need my key. You can keep the wig." Her voice relaxed, her lips all smiles. "Milena was at the wrong place, at the wrong time, as they say. I was days from leaving. A whole new world waiting for me. Bye, bye, Mrs. Russell, hello self-made millionaire Ruby Alexander." She seemed to talk to herself. "Look, I had to put Milena somewhere before I gave the Testarossa to Kyle. She died in her sleep—"

"In the trunk of your car?"

The phone rang again.

The smile disappeared from her face, and with her free hand she grabbed the phone, pulled it off the table, cord and all, and dropped it on the floor. Her eyes never left mine.

"Ruby, are you talking about the wrong mailbox key you sent me?"

"Oh, yes. That's the one. Silly mistake." The happy voice was back.

"I figured you accidentally mailed me your mailbox key, so I brought it back."

The anticipation that had lit up her face quickly disappeared. "You brought it back? Where?"

"To your house. You weren't home so I gave it to your neighbor across the street. You know, Mrs. Snoopy?" I watched the rainbow of suspicions color her expression. She bought it. I thought. She tapped her fingers on the tabletop where the phone used to be. I could almost hear her brain churning. True or false?

"Okey dokey." She let out a sharp giggle. "Let's pay Mrs. Snoopy a visit, shall we?"

"Uh—I can't. See? I can't wear shoes." I lifted my left foot to show her. I saw contempt on her face.

"Give it up. Your 'poor little me' may have done the trick on him, but it's over."

"Him?" It came out more as a sigh than a question, because somewhere deep in my brain I'd known the answer for a very long time.

"Nick." She said it. Her voice was a sweet whisper, the kind of dreamy awe reserved for idols, heroes...or the love of your life.

It was my turn to take a step toward Ruby.

"You bring sorrow to whoever cares about you."

She hit me with the fist holding the gun. I tasted blood inside my lip.

"I bring sorrow? You bitch! You Italian trash! He died because of you. He couldn't leave you."

"Couldn't or wouldn't?"

"Ahh!" She lunged, trying to hit me again. I grabbed her hand, attempting to get the gun away. My anger fueled my strength. I wanted to twist her arm behind her back the way they did in cop shows. I was so sure there weren't any bullets in the gun, I felt empowered.

I was wrong.

The gun fired. I heard glass shattering and Flash's cry pierced my ears and my heart. I punched Ruby's face with all my might. She fell back and hit her elbow against the table, "Fuck!" I heard the gun land on the travertine tile. I had my arm around her chest and my other arm firmly around her neck, but she stomped my shoeless left foot with her heel. I screamed and we ended up wrestling on the couch. I don't know who had the upper hand because my front door crashed open and Larry and Bob and God-knows-who-else came rushing in.

TWENTY-NINE

We sat in the same waiting room where I had been the day before, March nineteenth. Thinking about all that had happened the past twenty-four hours made my head spin. Kyle was out of jail. Ruby was on her way to jail. That was the most important change of all.

No broken bones, and my bruises would be better in a week, the doctor told me.

I let Larry take me to the emergency room because he said the police would need the report. Fine. I wanted to go home and get some sleep.

"I bet they'll reopen Tom Russell's death investigation."

"You think so?"

"I read the report when it happened, and I'm pretty sure the death was ruled accidental because Ruby claimed she'd never touched a gun before and had no idea how it worked. I don't remember the exact words. It would be interesting to see what kind of life insurance the man carried." Larry smiled and helped me to the car. "The crimes people do for money."

"There wasn't any money involved with poor Aunt Millie. Do you think she suffered?"

"Let it go, sweetie. Even if the story of her fall is true, she would have survived if taken to a hospital. Bonnie was telling me that the trunk and the passenger seat of the Testarossa had been washed with river water. Ruby must have gotten rid of the body, washed the trunk and the car seat, then made a U-turn to Palm Springs to switch cars with Kyle."

We drove in silence for a while. "I used to think she was mentally challenged because of the accident. She was smart enough to take the wig, ID and plant a fake suicide note."

"I have the feeling the note was real. Aunt Millie was getting ready to sign off." Larry put his hand on my knee. "There were sleeping pills in her purse. We found them in Ruby's car."

"We?"

"I was on my way to Santa Ana with Bob when the tip came in—the Ford Focus was spotted in your garage. A security guard made the call. We were lucky—you were lucky. First thing the guys did was take over the Focus. We knew Ruby was in the house because you didn't answer your phone. Before we could come up with a plan we heard the gunshot—"

"And you wrecked my front door."

"Hey, I saved your life." Larry enjoyed the sparring, I could tell.

"I could have saved my own life, thank you very much. Is the police department going to replace my door?"

"What? You're serious about this, aren't you?"

"Absolutely!"

"Fine. Tomorrow we go out, get you a new hat and a new door. Will that do it, or am I missing something?"

"I'll let you know after I pick up Flash and see the bill from the vet."

He pulled to the side of the road and stopped the car. His hand cupped my face. I felt the warmth of his breath on my throat and smelled his familiar aftershave. "How long before your lips are ready to kiss again?" he whispered in my ear.

I guided his hand inside my blouse. Before the back of the seat reclined, I caught a glimpse of the moon reflecting on the Pacific.

A note from Maria Grazia Swan

Gemini Moon was inspired by the death of a very good friend of mine. She died of a gunshot to the head. Her death was ruled accidental. The shooter? Her husband. This happened in 1990, in Southern California. I knew I had to write about it, I also knew I wanted to do it right.

Time went by, I wrote books and short stories. And one day I was ready. In Gemini Moon, the roles are reversed, the wife shoots the husband. Because of my strong friendship with the woman whose death inspired the story, I describe her as she really was in life, pretty, smart, funny, bubbly and full of love. R.I.P. Yvonne.

Thank you for reading us, if you have questions, suggestions, ideas, don't hesitate to reach out, I'm thrilled to hear from readers. And if you liked the book, would you please post a review? It's easy, only a few words would it and it means so much to us authors.

Ciao, Maria Grazia

A sneak peek at
Venetian Moon

One

Venice-Italy, October 2008
The heavy doors closed with a swoosh. I paused to survey the human wall squeezed behind the crowd barriers. Only strangers' eyes looked back

My hope to encounter a friendly smile, a familiar face faded.

I walked by the crowd of people waiting for disembarking passengers to clear customs, my hand steady on the rolling luggage, my head held high, my heart a heap of shards.

He is not here. What will I do?

I kept on walking. Damn autumn sun reflecting on the fountains outside the walls of glass caused my eyes to tear up.

I didn't ask for much. A hug, a comforting word. He promised.

I forgot how small the arrival terminal of Venice Marco Polo airport was. If not for the noise level, it felt like a tea parlor compared to Los Angeles International.

What could possibly be so important to keep him from meeting me?

"*Signora* York, *Signora* York."

I turned. A tall woman ran toward me. "*Signora* York, sorry to be late." She spoke Italian and for inexplicable reasons, I found it soothing.

Long legs inside knee high black boots and skin tight jeans, a dark sweater and a loose quilted vest same color as the sweater. As she approached I could tell the clothing was charcoal color, the hair a rusted brown. Who was she? I had no doubt, I never met the woman before.

"*Signora* York." Between words she made sucking noises, like small gasps. "Sorry to have you wait. There was an accident on the *autostrada*." She stopped and studied my face. "You don't know who I am, do you?"

I shook my head.

She offered her hand, "Pia. Pia Bartolomei, surely Kyle, your son, most have told you. About me—us. No?" It was her turn to shake her head, a smirk replaced the forced smile. "No, of course. So typical." She tried to take the suitcase handle from me, I resisted. "Where is Kyle?" I asked.

She fidgeted with her hair, a single braid resting on her right shoulder. "Roma. Cinecitta'. Last two days. He had no choice." Her voice laced with resentment.

Resentment for my presence or my son's absence?

We faced each other, this—Pia, a whole head above mine. Where does my son find these women? Always so tall. What's that thing he says? "Can I help it if I like roses with long stems?"

"*Signorina* Bartolomei, did Kyle—has my son told you where I should meet him?" *Awkward.*

"Please, call me Pia. I'm to drive you to the condo, he hopes to be able to come up to Venice in two days, after they wrap up the interior takes."

"You mean in two days he'll be completely done? I had no idea."

"No, not really. A few retakes are scheduled here, that's why he thought it would be easier for you to stay put. Jet lag and such."

We crossed the airport parking lot that always reminded me of large generic parking grounds like the ones around American Walmarts. The wheels of my suitcase made squeaky sounds. While the inside arrival space was packed with people, the parking lot looked empty. I visited Italy two years ago, but this was my first time landing at Marco Polo in six years. A glimpse of the Laguna and St Mark's *Campanile* delighted my eyes as the plane started its descent. I always felt sorry for first time visitors when they realized that Venice's airport was actually not in Venice.

I trailed Pia by a few steps. We didn't have a thing to talk about. She stopped by a two door faded green VW, clicked something in her hand and the hatchback opened. She waited, her eyes on me. *Got it.* I slid my suitcase into the back door of the car and she slammed it closed. A faded I heart NY sticker on the corner made me smile.

The tension between us palpable. When I turned to buckle the seat belt I noticed a lanyard dangling from the rearview mirror, a square badge attached to it. Even without my reading glasses I could see the name Pia Bartolomei. What really attracted my attention was the word above that. Large, dark blue letters spelled out PRESS. And then I remembered.

"*Mio Dio*, that's you, the girl from RAI TV. In California, at Kyle's hearing. You were doing a special about second-generation Italians in America."

She kept her hand on the ignition key without starting the car, and smiled. "He did tell you about me."

A long sigh.

I went on. "Yes, he did and I must say, Kyle was quite smitten, apparently he still is." I smiled back.

We went from silent strangers to gabbing friends thanks to a single word—PRESS. I asked her to call me Lella.

October hadn't affected the trees lining the access to the airport, perhaps the warm weather accounted for the green lingering on the branches. Anywhere but here this type of entrance would be considered more suitable for a high end private school rather than a public International airport. Then again Marco Polo was unique, built for modern comfort among splashes from the past, a statue here, a fountain there.

"So where is this condo? Is it Kyle's?" I asked

"Lella, I can't believe Kyle hasn't prepared you regarding the accommodations. The condo belongs to Cruz."

"Tom Cruise?" I assumed she mispronounced English names.

"Oh, no, no," A short laugh, "Manuel De La Cruz, you know—the actor?" She glanced at me sideways apparently astonished by my ignorance. The name meant nothing.

"Kyle and Cruz are working together. That's one of the reason they're sharing the condo. The place belongs to one of Cruz's...friends." Another laugh, more a snort than a laugh. "She hardly ever comes to Italy. Anyway, Cruz plays the long lost older brother. It would be correct to assume he is the main attraction as the movie title is *The Lost Heir*. I'm not saying Kyle's part isn't important, but Cruz is well known in Italy, while Kyle is new to the game."

"Game?"

"Yeah, you know, he doesn't have any major motion pictures in Italy yet. Cruz is a household name. This is not a reflection of talent, only of popularity among moviegoers." The last part was added in a hurry, as if making sure not to offend me. "By the way, Kyle sends a *telefonino* for you to use. I'm afraid American mobile phones do not work in Europe."

He did think about his mom after all.

We drove in the opposite direction from the arrows indicating Venezia. We entered a busy industrial area with many roads intersecting. Where were we headed? Pia's driving was a little rough. I'd forgotten about manual shift, it came back every time she changed gear. The signs Pia seemed to follow clearly stated Ravenna and Chioggia. That confused me.

"Pia, where is this condo? Isn't Venezia the other way?"

"We are driving to Chioggia, the miniature Venezia as the locals like to call it. This is no ordinary condo, it comes with its own story, and it's all connected to the film industry."

I didn't know what to say, too many sleepless nights and the horrible trip with so many change of planes because of my last minute decision to fly to Italy. I felt mentally exhausted, dazed.

She glanced at me. "The mother of the present owner was an extra in a French movie made in Chioggia. She had a major crush on Jean Paul Belmondo, the actor. Was there more than a crush? That was in the sixties, I wasn't even born."

I was.

"Anyway," Pia went on, "when the old palace used in one of the scene got remodeled, divided and sold she bought one of the apartments. Upon her death it became property of her only daughter who lives in France. The heiress apparently finds Chioggia too small and boring for her tastes, but she can't sell the place so she lets Cruz use it. I'm sure he knows how to show his appreciation."

The idle chatter kept my driver's attention occupied. For that I was thankful. The last thing I wished was for Pia to notice my state of turmoil and ask questions. Anything to keep me from facing the reason I boarded that flight to Venice.

ABOUT THE AUTHOR

Maria Grazia Swan was born in Italy, but this rolling stone has definitely gathered no moss. She lived in Belgium, France, Germany, in beautiful Orange County, California where she raised her family, and is currently at home in Phoenix, Arizona—but stay tuned for weekly updates of Where in the World is Maria Grazia Swan?

As a young girl, her vivid imagination predestined her to be a writer. She won her first literary award at the age of fourteen while living in Belgium. As a young woman Maria returned to Italy to design for—ooh-la-la—haute couture. Once in the U.S. and after years of concentrating on family, she tackled real estate. These days her time is devoted to her deepest passions: writing and helping people find happiness. Maria loves travel, opera, good books, hiking, and intelligent movies (if she can find one, that is). When asked about her idea of a perfect evening, she favors stimulating conversation, spicy Italian food and perfectly chilled Prosecco—but then, who doesn't?

Maria has written short stories for anthologies, articles for high profile magazines and numerous blogs tackling love and life. Her romantic suspense novels *Love Thy Sister* , *Bosom Bodies, Italian Summer, Ashes of Autumn, Best in Show* and *A Cat to Die For* are available at Amazon.com. She engaged her editorial and non-fiction skills for Mating Dance: Rituals for Singles Who Weren't Born Yesterday.

Website: http://www.mariagraziaswan.com
Contact Maria: mgsweb1@gmail.com
—or—touch base with her on Facebook.

Books by Maria Grazia Swan

Mina's Adventure series

Lella York series

Made in the USA
San Bernardino, CA
11 December 2016